As his face descended to hers, she looked wide-eyed up at him. "What are you . . ?" she whispered breathlessly. Before she could finish the question, she was crushed against his hard body, his lips were bruising hers with a fiercely punishing kiss. She was stunned first into frightened acquiescence but when his hand moved over her back pulling her closer, something of the untamed animal stirred in her own breast.

It was a moment of desperate frustration, when she knew she should be outraged, but could only go on clinging to him as if her life depended on it . . .

LOVE'S HARBINGER

Joan Smith

FAWCETT CREST • NEW YORK

A Fawcett Crest Book
Published by Ballantine Books
Copyright © 1987 by Joan Smith

Library of Congress Catalog Card Number: 87-90768

ISBN 0-449-20955-5

Manufactured in the United States of America

First Edition: July 1987

Chapter One

Lady Lynne sat, sipping a cup of cocoa while nibbling a macaroon, and wondered why she was suddenly putting on a little weight. She was still a decade from that sad time of life when she would turn gray and quarrelsome—her brindled hair was not frosted with white at all. Since Sir John's death she had begun having her gowns constructed in Paris, and at the moment she was upholstered in an extremely fashionable yellow sateen that made her look like a rutabaga. She was well aware of this and resented it deeply. But she was easily distracted from unpleasant thoughts, for she was basically an optimistic lady. What else could account for her volunteering every Season to find a *parti* for one or another of her country nieces? This year it was Lady Faith Mordain, her companion in cocoa and macaroons, who had been blasted off, or soon would be. Only it was very odd that Lord Thomas Vane had not come to call this afternoon as he was supposed to do. She sometimes feared that sly Lord Thomas meant to slip the leash. He had been behaving oddly lately. Still, it would not do to put such an idea into Faith's head, so she said, "Get the *Harbinger*, will you, dear? I sent Basset for it, and just heard him come in."

Lady Faith lifted a well-shaped brow and stared at her aunt with a pair of intelligent gray eyes. "I don't know why you read that scurrilous rag," she said, but she rose and went into the hall. Faith was tall and slender, and carried herself nobly as befitted the daughter of an earl.

1

Her short hair, black as jet, shone when she passed the window. Despite the small purse her father had sent to take care of wardrobe requirements, a decent toilette had been acquired for Faith. Fortunately, she looked best in rather plain gowns, which cost so much less to have made up than fancy ones. There was a serious air about the girl that made ribbons and furbelows ineligible.

Lady Lynne reached eagerly for the newspaper and explained to her niece, "I read it for Mam'selle Ondit's gossip column, my dear, like all the ladies. Mam'selle never misses a beat. Mind you, the *Harbinger* is finding its way into all the more enlightened homes. The gentlemen read it, too, for the hard political and money news. They do say Guy Delamar is becoming the conscience of England." She opened the paper at the gossip column and began to read avidly.

"Setting up in competition with William Cobbett," Faith replied, and resumed her seat.

Her eyes roamed the tables for something more informative than the *Harbinger*, but saw only *La Belle Assemblée*. She glanced at her aunt, drew a deep breath, and looked at the clock. Four-thirty. Thomas wouldn't be coming now. What could have happened to him? He had missed more than one appointment during the past week. It was his business venture with Mr. Elwood that acounted for it, no doubt. She had no adverse thoughts on this matter. If there was a flaw in her beloved Thomas, it was his lack of a fortune, but the investment company he had instituted would ercome that. It appeared to be succeeding even beyond Thomas's expectations. Hundreds of people wanted a share in it. Still, he might have let her know if he had a new investor to interview this afternoon.

But she could not be angry with him long. If it were not for Thomas, it would be back to the country for her, her one chance at winning a *parti* gone forever. Next year it would be Hope's turn. With four daughters to be disposed of, Lord Westmore allowed them only one chance each. The Mordain daughters were all named for virtues and were encouraged to pay special allegiance to their own particular one. She would have faith in Thomas, then.

Something had come up at the last minute. Tonight he would explain everything, when he walked through the door, wearing his reckless smile and looking so handsome her heart would do somersaults in her chest. How had she had the great fortune to catch the interest of the handsomest man in London? He might have had anyone, but he had chosen her, she who had no particular beauty and only a small fortune. Everyone had thought he would marry some undistinguished commoner with a fat dowry to allow him the carefree, dashing sort of life he favored, but there was an unexpected strength of character in him. "I shall bestow my name where I have already bestowed my heart," he had said. And with luck in his business venture, he would bestow a fortune as well.

Her Aunt Lynne put down the paper and emitted a girlish giggle. "Listen to this, Faith. 'The Honorable Margaret deVigne was lovely, as usual, in pink. No one likened her to a sow, which refutes the rumor that the English are uncharitable.' Oh, my, what a vitriolic pen Mam'selle has."

"I wonder if she's really French," Faith remarked idly.

"French? My dear, it is no secret that Delamar writes the column himself. *He* is Mam'selle Ondit."

"How would a person like Delamar learn the *on-dits* of society?" she scoffed. "Why doesn't he pick on the peccadilloes of his own class?"

"Why, he is accepted in the best saloons nowadays, though I have not had the pleasure of his acquaintance myself. Who would be interested to read that John Farmer or Tom Merchant had run off with his neighbor's wife? *That* is not news, except to their few friends and neighbors, who probably cannot read in the first place. Mr. Delamar knows the value of his betters and writes of the aristocracy. They say he's made a tidy fortune with this paper. I know I would never miss an issue." Her eyes

3

returned to the paper and soon a stifled shriek rose in her throat.

"What is it?"

"Listen to this, Faith. 'Investors in the Afro-Gold Investment Company are upset at the rumor that its founder, Lord Thomas Vane, is planning a protracted and highly secret visit abroad. This paper's investigation shows that the Afro-Gold Investment Company has not been registered, nor have shares been issued. More to follow.' I gave Thomas five thousand guineas to buy me shares! He means to take the money and run."

Faith looked at her aunt's face, which had turned snow white. In that white mask, her aunt's brown eyes flashed in horror, and she clutched the paper nervously in her fingers.

Faith also showed signs of severe agitation. Her eyebrows rose an eighth of an inch and she said firmly. "That's ridiculous! Thomas wouldn't do such a thing."

"He's been acting very havey-cavey ever since he took up with that Elwood fellow. Twice this week he missed an appointment. Before today, I mean."

"And both times he was busy with his investors," Faith reminded her.

"What shall I do? I'm sending Basset straight off with a note to Thomas."

In her distracted state, she went after the butler, then returned to pick up the paper and read the item again. "It's true, I know it's true. I feel it in my bones. I never did trust Thomas Vane above half. Five thousand pounds! I am ruined!" This was a gross exaggeration, but the loss of five thousand pounds would certainly require a few unpleasant stringencies in the comfortable Lynne household.

"Auntie, calm yourself. You can't take the word of that horrid old paper. Thomas would *never* do such a thing. It is a cur's trick to increase the paper's circulation. There is nothing Delamar wouldn't sink to."

"Delamar is *always* right, Faith," her aunt countered. "They call him the Bloodhound of Fleet Street. I'm going to see him. He wouldn't dare print an item like this without some proof."

"Wait till Basset returns. It is all a hum, you'll see."

"Get your bonnet and pelisse. I'm calling for the carriage, and when Basset returns, we shall go to the office of the *Harbinger*. I'll have my money back from Vane if I have to beat it out of him with my bare hands."

Faith didn't stir a finger. She sat calmly waiting for Basset's return while her aunt had their bonnets and pelisses brought down. At least she *looked* calm, though even a lady trained in the virtue of faith was prey to one little doubt. It was close to half an hour before Basset entered. He wore a long face and came in shaking his head.

"His lordship's flat is empty. I hammered at the door for five minutes and then asked around at other flats. Nobody's seen him since this morning. Lord Thomas left with a trunk."

"Impossible!" Faith said bravely, but her heart trembled within her. Had she lost Thomas, then? She had felt from the beginning that her luck was too good to be true—that Thomas was too good to be true, and much too good for her.

Lady Lynne gave her niece a hard, accusing glare, though it was she who had pushed this match forward. She set Faith's bonnet on her head and handed her her pelisse. "I told you so!" she said, and strode angrily out the door.

Neither lady spoke much as the carriage drove them to the Strand, eastward toward Fleet Street. Though Lady Faith found much to admire in Samuel Johnson, she could not agree with him that Fleet Street was the most cheerful scene in the world; it was only the noisiest and the busiest. It was the highway from Charing Cross to St. Paul's and was full of traffic, wagons and pedestrians as well as coaches. On the sidewalk, men streamed in and out of taverns and coffeehouses and browsed at bookstalls. Boys no older than eleven or twelve were in abundance, looking remarkably black of face and hands.

The carriage slowed down at Printing House Square, a handsome building fronted with iron palings.

"Is it possible Mr. Delamar has amassed such a vast fortune from his rag that he works here?" Faith asked.

"Widgeon! That is where Mr. Walters puts out the *Times*," her aunt said.

Their driver only stopped to inquire for directions, then turned into a back alley where the buildings were much less grand. The *Harbinger* sign was blazoned in white on black paint across a row of low, wooden buildings. Lady Faith felt it was no place for ladies to venture, but her aunt was adamant.

They lifted up their skirts to avoid the dusty clutter of the road and went to the door. The first sight that greeted them inside was a sign proclaiming ADVERTISING OFFICE. The door was closed and no light shone within. The dim shadows suggested that the building was empty. One of those extremely dirty boys seen in the street came flying through the front door and gave them a saucy look.

"Who are you looking for, ladies?" he chirped.

"We would like a word with Mr. Delamar," Lady Lynne informed him. "Where is everyone? And why are you as black as the ace of spades, lad? Go and wash yourself."

"This paint don't come off. It's ink. I'm a printer's devil!" he said proudly. "The rag's put to bed. There won't be no one here till tomorrow morning. Just let me run up and see if Guy's still in his flat."

He ran off to the rear of the office, turned, and disappeared. They heard the echo of his little feet flying up the stairs. Soon he came back to invite them up to see Mr. Delamar. It was necessary to lift their skirts once more, for the narrow, wooden staircase wore no carpeting save dust.

"It's strange Mr. Delamar lives in a hovel when he has reputedly made his fortune," Faith mentioned.

Her aunt pulled in her lips and said, "I begin to wonder if the stories of his success haven't been exaggerated."

Mr. Delamar's living in such squalor gave both ladies

the courage to take high ground with him. They tapped at a derelict wooden door, and another of those ebony boys admitted them. The chamber they entered was no better than the rest. A brown horsehair sofa was the main furnishing. The presence on it of a pillow and blankets indicated that it served as not only sofa but bed. An undistinguished desk littered with papers, a chair, and lamps completed the furnishings. The windows bore no draperies, only a coat of grime.

"Have a seat. Guy'll be out as soon as he's finished shaving," the boy said.

They looked at the sofa and elected to remain standing. From the rear of the flat, a sound of whistling carried easily to their ears. Soon the echo of a razor being stropped followed it, then water running and other indications that Mr. Delamar was making a leisurely toilette. Lady Lynne was not a patient woman, and when two minutes had passed, she walked to the near end of the corridor, raised her voice, and called imperiously, "We are waiting for you, Mr. Delamar."

"I'll be with you in a minute. Help yourself to a glass of wine," he called back in a deep, authoritative voice.

Lady Lynne ignored the offer but said sotto voce to her niece, "At least he *sounds* like a gentleman."

"A pity he doesn't act like one," Faith snipped.

Whatever his social status, Lady Lynne had to acknowledge that Mr. Delamar was certainly extremely striking when she first clamped a lustful eye on him. She was partial to handsome gentlemen of all ages, and the detail of Delamar's being at least a decade younger than her own forty years in no way invalidated him as a potential flirt. He had an air of *diablerie* that she soon interpreted as a preference for older ladies. She quickly assessed the elegant jacket that fit his body like paper on a wall, and while it was not the work of London's premier tailor, Weston, it was not from the hand of the outlandish Stutz either. Scott, she thought, was responsible for the jacket. But who or what was responsible for Mr. Delamar—that dashing, angry, savagely handsome man

7

who stared down a generous nose at her from a pair of topaz tiger's eyes? He took a step forward, strengthening the first impression of a tiger.

There was something of the pounce of a jungle cat in his stride as he advanced, his hand extended. Lady Lynne felt her heart quicken when she put her hand in his and had it squeezed quite mercilessly. She examined a pair of prominent cheekbones that looked as bony as elbows. Across the top of the left one, a long, thin scar was fading from pink to white. It gave him a rakish, dangerous air that reinforced her excitement. To add to his savage looks, his skin was bronze. Was he part Indian? Delamar didn't sound like it, but that blue-black hair and bronze skin could not be English. England did not produce such wild fauna as this man.

Faith noticed that her aunt had turned mute and rushed in with their names. "This is my aunt, Lady Lynne, and I am Lady Faith Mordain," she said haughtily. She was subjected to another crushing grip, the fire from the topaz tiger's eyes, and to a smile that had been absent from his greeting to the older lady. It was not a sweet or gentle smile. It did nothing to mitigate the sensation of being in a small room with a savage. It merely made her fear that the savage might eat her. It was a strangely predatory smile.

"Mr. Delamar, at your service, ladies," he said, and waved a hand to the dusty horsehair sofa. Such was their state of distraction that they pushed the blankets and pillow aside and sat down. He pulled a chair up beside them, leaned forward, and said in a calm, businesslike way, "What can I do for you?"

When Lady Lynne found a voice, her niece observed that it was her low, crooning voice usually reserved for seduction. In a flash she foresaw that the interview would not go as planned, unless she made it go that way. "We've come about that naughty article in your paper, Mr. Delamar," Lady Lynne said, coquettishly waving a finger.

There was a bantering light in the tiger's eyes. "Which one, ma'am? If you are a regular reader, you must know they're all naughty."

"Oh, you *are* wicked! I read the *Harbinger* as regularly as my Bible."

"What, only once a year?" he replied, roasting her, and let his eyes rove to Faith, who glared.

"What a wicked man you are! But it is the article about Lord Thomas Vane I am referring to," her aunt continued.

"He gouged you, too, did he? I wish I could tell you it's untrue, but it appeared in the *Harbinger*, so we must take it for gospel. Do you have something to add to the story? I'm collecting the names of the victims for the next issue. You'll be in good company, Lady Lynne. How much did you lose?"

Before her aunt could reply, Lady Faith took her courage in hand and set the conversation on its proper course. "We aren't here to submit our names for publication in the *Harbinger*, Mr. Delamar. That catastrophe must be avoided by all means. We want to know where you heard this libelous rumor," she demanded.

He slowly turned his head to Faith and regarded her for a long moment. When he finally spoke, it was not to answer her question but to get a firmer grip on the identity of his callers. "Lady Faith Mordain—that rings a bell. Ah, now I see! Please allow me to offer my condolences, ma'am. You are Lord Thomas's greatest victim. The others have lost only money. You have lost your . . . heart?" His bright, inquisitive eyes seemed to be boring inside her head. "Have you, by any chance, lost money as well?"

"Certainly not! Lord Thomas has stolen nothing. I must insist on knowing the source of that rumor you published, sir."

"I make it a rule never to divulge my sources, ma'am. That is an excellent way to dry up the spring. You may be assured the information is accurate. He's given you the bag, has he? Shabbed off, and the wedding only two weeks away."

"You must not print such a thing!" Lady Lynne exclaimed.

"I shan't," he assured her, "till I learn from an unimpeachable source that it's true. Is it?"

9

"No, it is not," Lady Faith said firmly.

"Then you know where he is?" Delamar asked sharply. "If you know something that proves Lord Thomas innocent, it would be to his advantage—and your own—to arrange an interview between him and myself. I know he had a partner, a Mr. James Elwood. It's possible he's only Elwood's dupe," he said doubtfully.

"Lord Thomas is no one's dupe!" Faith objected.

Delamar regarded her thoughtfully. "He is either a dupe or a knave, madam. Take your pick. I should think *you*, of all people, would be grateful to me for discovering it before you make the mistake of marrying him."

"He is nothing of the sort! How *dare* you libel a gentleman's character! I insist you write a retraction at once."

Delamar listened, unmoved. "I accused him of nothing. Better reread my column; I only report the facts. It is a fact that Lord Thomas Vane and Mr. James Elwood have taken in over two hundred thousand pounds in subscriptions to the Afro-Gold Investment Company. It is also fact that the company is not registered, and that Lord Thomas has left the city and Mr. Elwood has run to ground—hidden somewhere or other. I can tell you at what discreet, out-of-the-way travel agency Lord Thomas made his travel plans, if you don't know it already."

"Where is it?" Lady Lynne asked eagerly.

Delamar turned his attention to the older lady. His expression stiffened to uncompromising firmness. "There's no free ride, ladies. My business isn't giving information away—I sell or barter it. What can you tell me in exchange for my news?"

"We haven't an idea where he is," Lady Lynne admitted. "He didn't keep an appointment with Lady Faith this afternoon. He's missed a few of them lately. I sent my butler over to his flat and learned that he's flown the coop."

Lady Faith was stirred to defend her fiancé. "He's gone home to his father's estate. He wasn't feeling well," she invented.

"Can I quote you on that?" Delamar asked.

"No!"

Lady Lynne shook her head. "It is all a hum, Mr. Delamar. She has no more idea where he is than you have. It's true, then; I've been swindled."

"How much did you subscribe?" Delamar asked.

"Don't tell him," Lady Faith warned her aunt. "He'll print it in that scurrilous paper! I thought we came here to object to the story." Looking at her aunt, she missed the sneer that alit on Delamar's face.

"Object?" Lady Lynne asked, astonished. "*I* came to find out if it was true. It obviously is, goose. We must break off the engagement at once."

"No!" Faith gasped. "No, it—it cannot be true. Mr. Delamar is mistaken. Mr. Delamar, I think you might, just this once, divulge your source. I am very closely involved in this affair."

"As I said, tit for tat. You give me an exclusive on Lord Thomas, the sort of intimate thing only a fiancée would know, and I'll tell you what I've discovered to date."

She stared at him as though he were a snake. "You actually expect me to divulge intimate secrets about Lord Thomas? You must be mad!"

"I'm not talking about how he makes love, though it would charm Mam'selle Ondit's readers. I only want to know if you have anything concrete to offer in his defense—or to substantiate his guilt," he added maliciously.

"He is not guilty!"

Delamar rose and began to pace the room. "Before you go naming a church after him, consider the evidence." As he walked, he ticked off points on his long, tanned fingers. "He did not register the Anglo-Gold Company, he took in over two hundred thousand pounds, he's tipped his investors the double, he's failed to show up for appointments with his fiancée, he's even gulled your aunt. If that does not at least raise a doubt, you are dangerously unsuspicious. I wonder if you will be as lenient when he doesn't show up at St. George's in Hanover Square for the wedding. 'Lady Faith Jilted by Faithless Lover.' That should make good reading."

"You wouldn't dare!" She gasped.

"I will! But only if it happens, of course. I print nothing but facts. And I've never printed a retraction in my life, so if that was your only business, ladies . . . I am rather busy." He rose and looked impatiently at the door.

Lady Faith glared harder than before, then turned to her aunt. "Come along, Auntie. We're wasting our time. We will want to stop at our solicitor's office before going home."

A slow smile crept across Mr. Delamar's face, lifting his scar and crinkling the corners of his eyes. He came forward and offered Faith his hand to help her up from the sofa. She pointedly ignored it. "If that is meant to intimidate me, you're wasting your time. Save your blunt. You have no case. I suggest you follow your aunt's advice and write up a notice cancelling the engagement. Shall I do it for you?"

Faith pulled away. "If you print that lie, then I *will* sue, I promise you. I shall marry Lord Thomas Vane, and he is not a thief."

"I didn't say he was."

"You implied it! And you believe it."

"True, but then what do you care what *I* believe?"

"I don't! Come along, Auntie. We cannot expect Mr. Delamar to understand that a *gentleman* does not steal." On this cutting phrase, she allowed her eyes to rove around his cramped and ugly saloon. They still wore an expression of deep disgust when she allowed them to flicker over Mr. Delamar. "Good day." She carefully lifted her skirts and stalked out.

It was extremely disobliging of her aunt not to follow her. She felt a perfect fool, waiting for her in the hall.

Before leaving, Lady Lynne gave Delamar her hand. "Please keep in touch if you learn anything further about Lord Thomas. About that exchange of information . . . I am Lady Faith's chaperone. I know as much as she does. What is it you want to know?"

"Where he is."

"I can't help you there. He wouldn't dare to go home

12

to his father and, of course, he was not feeling ill at all. Do you plan to go after him?"

"Of course, and Mr. Elwood, too. This is the juiciest story I've come across in an age. And it happens I have other business at—in the same direction."

"When will you leave?"

"The only reason I'm still here is that I've been scurrying around, trying to get a lead on Elwood. There are rumors he's still in town, though he's not at his flat. I want to find out if Lord Thomas ran off with the whole lot or split it with Elwood. I don't see why Elwood would be hiding if he were totally innocent, but still it's Lord Thomas who has flown, and flight is usually taken as prima facie evidence of guilt. I'll be leaving around nine. The girl must know something, don't you think? She could help us, if she would."

"She's as stubborn as a mule, but I'll try my hand at pumping her for news. Why don't you drop around my place before you leave London? I might have something for you by then. She might have an idea where we could find Elwood at least. He was out with her and Thomas a few times."

"I was wondering if she plans to give you the slip and follow her Thomas. It's possible, I suppose. Is it a love match?"

Lady Lynne drew a thoughtful breath and settled on uncompromising vagueness. "They're fond of each other. Love will grow in time."

"You must be alluding to the old cliché that absence makes the heart grow fonder. I shouldn't think a vacuum the likeliest ambience for the sprouting of love. But then he won't really leave a vacuum behind, will he? He'll leave a trail of pain and mortification."

"And empty bank balances!" Lady Lynne added tartly.

"There are several that will be emptier than yours, Lady Lynne, though to steal from a friend carries a special sort of odium even for a nobleman," he said with a bold sneer that sent shivers of delight up her spine. "I'll drop by Berkeley Square some time before nine."

13

"Oh, you know where I live." She smiled.

"Knowing things is my business. I never did find out why such a charming young lady as yourself hasn't remarried—yet. Two years since you were widowed. London bachelors are slow-tops."

"Oh, you really are wicked!" she crooned, and tapped his fingers playfully, then darted off to meet her niece.

Mr. Delamar strolled to the window to watch them enter their carriage. There was a glow in his topaz eyes, but it was not a glow of admiration for Lady Lynne, who felt she had engaged his interest. He thought her a fat, silly old fool who might easily be led into revealing anything she knew, only he feared she knew even less than himself. It was a glow of suspicion directed at Lady Faith Mordain. Why was she so insistent that Lord Thomas was innocent? She didn't look like a fool. There was intelligence in those large gray eyes. Intelligence and anger and pride. The lady was stung at her public humiliation. A woman scorned might be led to help him, if he handled her properly. But he had always found the proud aristocracy difficult to handle. They stuck together like burrs, spreading their noble mantle over their own. He'd probably never get to the bottom of this Lord Thomas affair, but he'd give it his best effort. It was a personal crusade, almost a vendetta, that he bring Lord Thomas to justice. Even if he hadn't been the proprietor and editor of the *Harbinger*, he would have hounded Lord Thomas to the grave. He was sorry Lady Faith must be spattered in the fray, it she were innocent, but it wouldn't deter him.

Lord Thomas had chosen some of his victims poorly. He wouldn't get away with the life savings of Buck and Eddie. The Lady Lynnes of the world were of less interest to him, though of course they enhanced the interest of the story. But that his own buddies, who had risked their lives for England, should be duped by a Lord Thomas was not to be borne.

He was interrupted by the appearance of a printer's devil behind him. "What's up then, Guy?" the fellow asked.

"My dander. Call for my rig, Joey. If anything important comes up, I'll be at my house before I leave town."

"The new place?"

"That's right, in Piccadilly."

"Setting up as a regular nabob, eh, Guy?"

"Why not? I'm as good as the rest of them."

"Better."

"Toadeater." Guy laughed, and tossed him a golden boy.

Chapter Two

"It was a waste of time going there," Lady Faith said when they were back in the carriage, returning to Berkeley Square. "I, for one, place no credence in the story of that impertinent scandalmonger, Delamar." She might as well have been talking to herself for all the attention her aunt paid her.

Lady Lynne drew a deep sigh and asked in a soupy voice, "Did you notice his eyes? And that scar—from a duel, I daresay."

"More likely he got his head caught in a dustbin when he was rooting for a story." Again she was ignored.

"And his shoulders—they dwarf an ordinary man's." Then the dame reluctantly turned her mind to business. If her niece knew anything at all about Thomas's movements, it was necessary to squeeze the information out of her. "This Elwood fellow, Faith, you met him, I think?"

"Yes, a few times in the park, with Thomas. I didn't much care for him. I have no idea where he lived, but we met him once at his office on Tottenham Court Road just north of Great Russell. Thomas despised him. Of course it is Elwood who took the money."

"You should have told Mr. Delamar so!"

"I'm sorry we ever went to see him. He won't listen to reason. Let the bloodhound do his own sniffing."

"You forget I have five thousand pounds in that nonexistent company, my dear. You owe it to *me*, if not to

Thomas's erstwhile reputation, to do what you can to find him. Perhaps when I tell you Thomas tried to get his hands on *your* dowry as well, it will open up your eyes. Fortunately, your papa would not hear of it. I only wonder he didn't wait till he had married you, then run off with your pittance as well as mine.''

"This gives me the megrims. I hope we don't have to attend that rout party this evening?''

"I am not up to it,'' her aunt said, though it was not the megrims that would keep her away. She was on thorns for Mr. Delamar's visit and planned to entertain him without Lady Faith to chaperone them. She wished the girl farther away than upstairs in her bed and proceeded to convince her of her duty. ''Of course you must attend the rout, Faith. It is as good as an indictment of Thomas if you shab off.''

"How can I go? Everyone will be staring and talking. It will be horrid.''

"That is precisely why you must go, to give the lie to the rumors in case Mr. Delamar finds the money and we can wrap the whole affair up in clean linen. Tell everyone what you told Mr. Delamar, that Thomas was feeling poorly and went home for a rest. I cannot go, but I shall write a note to Mrs. Coates and send you off to her early, before she gets away. She will be happy to take you and save her own horses. You need do no more than put in an appearance. Come home as early as you like—any time after ten.''

Lady Faith's first instinct was to object, but a second thought showed her the possibility of helping Thomas. It was an excellent chance to get away from her chaperone for an hour to do a little investigating of her own. There was no point in going to Thomas's flat or to Mr. Elwood's, but that office on Tottenham Court Road . . . Mr. Delamar didn't know about it. She was sure she would find some evidence there to exonerate Thomas. He would be revealed as a flat, of course, taken in by Elwood, but better an honest dupe than a criminal.

She gave a resigned sigh and said, "Oh, very well, if you think I should."

The ladies went through the farce of sitting down to dinner. When Lady Lynne's appetite was up, she was an excellent trencherman, but that evening she was able to manage no more than half a pheasant and a dish of peas, though she was tempted back into appetite by the fresh strawberries and clotted cream served for dessert. Lady Faith's appetite was quenched by foreboding and her chaperone's ranting praise of Mr. Delamar. He was by turns a tiger, a noble savage, and once "an extraordinary specimen of virility."

"He certainly lives like a savage in that dismal hut above his shop," Faith pointed out for her aunt's edification.

"Not shop, my dear! A newspaper proprietor is head and shoulders above a merchant. Why, Fleet Street is a famous breeding ground for titles. I daresay he will be Lord Delamar before too long if he keeps his nose clean and learns to support the Tories. Then he will move into a respectable establishment. A man has to cut a few corners when he is getting started on his career."

Lady Lynne realized that Lord Thomas was lost as a husband for Faith and, with a mind to her duty, took the girl upstairs to enliven her toilette on the off chance that she might yet, in the two weeks of the Season that remained to her, make another catch. Faith, while not aspiring to the title of Incomparable, was by no means an antidote. She possessed that element rarer and more prized than ordinary beauty: she had countenance. Indeed, she had so much of it that it almost amounted to a flaw. Composure was all very well, but it ought to be ruffled at times; for instance, when a particularly eligible *parti* approached. Not Lady Faith; she would remain calm if her petticoats caught fire.

It never occurred to Lady Lynne that this monumental calm might be caused by shyness, for Faith tried very hard to conceal it. She forced herself to speak up, but getting much liveliness into her expression was beyond her.

Her worry about Thomas, however, was nearly enough to unsettle her sangfroid that evening. Her gray eyes sparkled and a blush of color stained her cheeks. The provincial hairdo she had worn to London had long since been revised to a more stylish Méduse coiffure, and her gown, though not much embellished with lace or ribbons, was exquisitely cut. The jonquil shade of Italian crepe, which had seemed at first too pale, looked very well this evening.

"That Fraser lad who used to dangle after you, Faith— if he makes a rapprochement this evening, don't cut him. He is only a junior member of the diplomatic corps, but he's young. He may go somewhere yet."

"At least he won't be going to Mordain Hall, where I'll end up if—" Faith began, then stopped in midspeech. She must not even think such things.

Lady Lynne laughed gaily and tried to reassure her. "Don't you believe it. I nabbed a viscount for your cousin Emily the last week of the Season, and I'll do as well for you yet. I won't have my record spoiled by that demmed Thomas Vane."

The niece was ushered out the door, and Lady Lynne bolted upstairs to add a touch of rouge to her cheeks and to put a very pretty, very long mohair shawl on her shoulders, for there was no denying that her waist had achieved such proportions that it was best concealed.

While Lady Lynne awaited the arrival of Mr. Delamar, Faith invented a tale to satisfy the groom that she must make a short stop on Tottenham Court Road before going to the rout. Her haughty mien and unexceptionable behavior to date gave John Groom no grounds for suspicion, though he did find it odd. But then the servants all knew that odd things were afoot vis-à-vis Lord Thomas and Lady Faith.

She hardly knew what she might find in Mr. Elwood's office, but her hope was that the money would be there. She had to accept that Thomas had left town—freely,

19

too—for he had packed his trunk and had been alone. No pistol or knife had been at his back. But if she could at least prove that he had not run off with the money, the marriage would go forth. What worried her considerably was her aunt's belief that Thomas *had* taken it. How could she believe such a thing? Thomas was carefree and sometimes a trifle unreliable about keeping appointments, but it was a long jump from there to call him a thief. Of course he was always short of money—what younger son was not? He owed his tailor and probably a few gambling debts, but his father planned to take care of all that when they married.

Tottenham Court Road was not in the elegant part of London familiar to debutantes. Faith felt a twinge of fear when she was let down into an unkempt shadowy street and approached the building where she and Thomas had once met Mr. Elwood. He had only one room in a corner of it. The front door was locked, of course. That was the first obstacle, and naturally the office door inside would also be locked. Mr. Elwood's office window looked out on the south side, so she ventured to the side of the building to try for access there. The groom came after her, warning her away from the dark alley.

"I must get inside. It is a matter of—of life and death," she asserted. "Can you pry that window open for me?"

"Let me call in Bow Street," John Groom suggested.

"That wouldn't do, Nubbins," she answered simply, but he understood that secrecy was vital and helped her. He also got the lantern from the carriage to aid in her search and suggested that she draw the curtains for privacy's sake.

"I'll keep an eye peeled here and come to your rescue if you have company," he offered.

"Thank you, Nubbins," she said as calmly and politely as though he were a footman handing her a glass of ratafia. Then Nubbins gave her a boost to allow her to scramble through the window into Mr. Elwood's office.

As her eyes adjusted to the darkness, she noticed that

the places of concealment in the single room were few. There were three chairs, the large cubbyhole desk, a coat tree, and a row of cupboards along one wall. The lantern showed her the outlines of these furnishings, and she went directly to the desk. She was pleasantly surprised when the drawers slid open easily, but when she looked in at their emptiness, she knew why Elwood hadn't bothered to lock them. Next she went to the cupboards. The lamp resting on the desk behind her threw long, menacing shadows on the wall. The office was perfectly still; you could hear a pin drop or your own breaths suspended on the air. The cupboard held some record books, which she took to the desk to peruse. She was reading a list of contributors to the Afro-Gold Investment Company when she heard a soft sound in the hall beyond the locked door, and her heart raced in fear. The sound was so slight that she at first mistook it for a stray cat or a gust of wind. As she listened, the sounds came closer and then stopped at the door.

Was it Nubbins, come to see if she was safe? She was about to call when it darted into her head that it might be Mr. Elwood. She hastily blew out the lantern and crouched behind the desk. She could feel the current from the open window and gauged her chances of getting out before he came in. They were slight, as she would require the chair to reach the window and a key was already turning in the lock. There was nothing for it but to stand up and face him, then. Yet when the key did not open the door easily, she hesitated. It might be anyone . . . a common thief who would slide a knife between her ribs before Nubbins came to her aid. The key turned, the door opened, and someone came in, closed the door quietly behind him, and turned the lock. The locking of the door was more frightening than the rest. He wasn't locking himself in. Did he already know she was there? A cold sweat broke out on her forehead and she felt her skin turn to gooseflesh.

From her hiding place behind the desk, she saw a dark shadow move and realized that someone was coming toward her but so softly she couldn't gauge the direction. Even the shadow had disappeared. Her breath caught in her lungs while she waited, looking helplessly at the window, which was too high for her to jump out of, and then at the locked door, where the unknown person blocked her exit. It seemed she waited a long time, wondering why the person didn't move, didn't do something or say something. Who could it be? Elwood wouldn't have to act so secretively. Was it—could it possibly be Thomas, come to try to extricate himself? Her nerves were screaming, and if that unknown presence didn't do something very soon, she would scream, too.

When the intruder at last moved, he moved so silently and swiftly it caught her unawares. The first intimation she had of it was the feel of cold steel against her temple. It froze her to the very marrow of her bones. "Nice and easy now, stand up, and no tricks." The voice was soft as silk—a mere susurrus, low-pitched and as menacing as the pistol muzzle that seared her flesh.

"Light the lantern," he said. "Let's have a look at you, miss." How did he know she had a lantern? How did he know she was a "miss"—he hadn't touched her. The man was magic.

She rose, trembling, and reached for the lantern. "I don't have a tinderbox," she said in a nervous, breathless voice. But she had the lantern in her hand and realized it made an excellent weapon. Without further delay, she raised it and struck out at her captor. She knew exactly where his head was, for he had just spoken. So how was it possible she missed him and swiped empty air with the lantern?

A light laugh floated from behind her—from a different direction than before—yet the pistol was still against her temple. "Tch, tch, Lady Faith! Mind your manners!" Were there two of them? No, only one had come in. How did he know who she was? Her heart pinched in fear as she realized that whoever was here she was no match for him. The man was directly behind her now; so near she felt the heat of his body against her back. She felt one arm go

22

around her waist, not with any amorous intent, but only to feel around the desk's surface for the tinderbox, which he shoved toward her fingers.

"Light the lantern," he ordered.

Her fingers trembled so badly she had to make three strikes of the steel against flint before she could ignite the charred linen and then the lantern. Again that long arm brushed past her waist, picked up the lantern, lifted it high, and then stood back. Feeling as if she were in a nightmare, she turned slowly to see who she had to deal with and found herself staring into the slightly slanted yellow eyes of Mr. Delamar. They glowed like the eyes of a wild animal in the dark. His high cheekbones stood out prominently in the shaft of light that shone up from the lantern. She could even distinguish the long, thin scar. He wore a perfectly diabolical expression.

"You!" she spat contemptuously.

"Good evening, Lady Faith." He performed a brief parody of a bow. "You must be lost. I didn't expect to see you so far from the West End. I trust I didn't frighten you?"

"You scared me to death!"

"Surely you exaggerate—you look more lively than when we first met. A little fear is becoming to you, and good for the constitution as well. Are you alone?"

As the fear dissipated, she assumed her more usual façade of stiff politeness. "The groom is waiting outside."

"I am impressed at your daring. Lord Thomas must be something quite out of the ordinary to lead you so far from the path of propriety. Hiding his light under a thimble, no doubt," he added with an ironical smile. "I expect we're both looking for the same thing. Did you have any luck?"

"No."

"Where have you looked?"

"In the desk and the cupboards. There's nowhere else to search."

"They didn't waste much blunt in putting up a good front, did they?"

"That seems to be the style in business nowadays," she answered tartly, remembering his own office.

He gave her a lazy smile and said, "Your point, madam. I would have space about me that is lean, to misquote the Bard." He then proceeded to search those same places Faith had, with more thoroughness but with no better success. "I'd say offhand he doesn't plan to return. The only thing he left behind is the record of purchasers and the lease for the office. A three-month lease. That pretty well tells the story—it expires the first of June, so Elwood has flown as well as Lord Thomas." She glared at him, but did not deign to point out his error. "Come, I'll take you home."

"I am not going home. I am on my way to a rout party." She picked up the lantern.

He placed the records under one arm, put his other hand on her elbow, and led her out, leaving the door unlocked behind them. "A rout party? I admire your courage, ma'am. Grace under pressure is an admirable trait. Is Lady Lynne waiting in the carriage? She must be planning to break our appointment."

"What appointment?" Faith demanded suspiciously.

"We have planned a tête-à-tête for this evening. I had some hopes you were to be included. I'm running a little late," he said, and pulled out a pocket watch. "Eight-twenty-five."

Faith looked at the clock on the wall and corrected him. "It's only eight-twenty."

He didn't even bother to look at the clock. "It's wrong. My watch is always right. I lead a split-second life," he said, and returned the timepiece to his pocket. It had an unusual fob that looked like a twisted piece of some dark metal. "I'll return you to Lady Lynne."

"She isn't with me. I'm going with a friend—I have to stop at her place." She looked at him uncertainly, disliking to ask a favor. "Actually, my aunt doesn't know I'm here. I would appreciate it if you didn't tell her."

"Then you should treat me more civilly, milady. I don't usually perform favors for people who try to bash me over the head."

"I didn't know who you were."

His feline eyes shot a mocking smile at her "Would it have made a difference?" he asked.

"Yes, I would have taken more careful aim, Mr. Delamar."

They reached her carriage, and he opened the door. "You still wouldn't have hit me." He laughed. "Beau Douro trained his guerrillas better than that."

Her head flew up in surprise. "What? Were you with Wellington in the Peninsula?" she asked.

"I've been many places, including Spain. Do try, if you can, to close your mouth. It is unflattering that you are so shocked at my being an—a soldier. Besides, open-mouthed ladies look so very witless, don't you agree?"

She closed her mouth, only to pull her lower lip between her teeth. Faith had the greatest admiration for military gentlemen, and she knew that those who had been with Wellington in the Peninsular War had been outstandingly fearless. "Not shocked, only surprised," she said. Embarrassment lent a softer tone to her voice and a becoming air of uncertainty to her manner. "I should have guessed by your complexion . . ."

"Ah, no, that only told you I am part blackamoor."

"What was your position in the army?"

"I always like to be in the forefront of any endeavor when trouble is brewing," he answered with studied obtuseness.

Not an officer then, she surmised, and changed the subject. "How did you know I was there in the office? And how did you know it was me? Even before I lit the lantern, you used my name."

"I smelled the burning oil. Lanterns don't light up by themselves, and when I was close to you, I recognized your perfume—a light lilac scent. Of course many ladies use that fragrance, but you *did* speak before I was certain it was you."

25

"You seemed to move around so quickly, too, like a cat."

"As I said, I am trained in warfare. Even a lady has been known to pull a trigger, so I was a little cautious. I am sorry if I frightened you, Lady Faith. I'll let you get on to your party now. Your aunt will tell you what plans I have to retrieve—er, the money," he finished, and was sorry to terminate their conversation on that reminder of Lord Thomas.

She pokered up immediately. "Good evening, Mr. Delamar."

He closed the door and the carriage drew away. Her stop had made her late in calling on Mrs. Coates, but by luck the dame had not left home yet, so Lady Faith avoided the unpleasantness of having to enter the party unattended. It was bad enough without that. She was the object of much interest, a little ill-concealed pity, but no rush of attention from chivalrous gentlemen. It was mainly dowagers who quizzed her about Lord Thomas. Her rehearsed speech was repeated so often that she was tired of it. In the end, she took a glass of wine and slipped into the vacant library to await the time when she could reasonably ask Mrs. Coates to leave.

She went to the farthest, darkest corner of the room and sat alone in the shadows, thinking. Mr. Elwood and Thomas had run off. It seemed she was the only woman in London who believed Thomas was innocent, but she still clung to the notion that Thomas had been tricked into behaving so foolishly. It was Elwood who was the creator of this wretched scheme. The whole idea was his; Thomas had said he had only been invited in to permit Mr. Elwood access to people who could afford to buy the shares—and possibly to be the scapegoat when Elwood fled? This new idea began to intrigue her. Of course, Thomas was a scapegoat! When he found out he'd been used, he'd come back and tell the whole story. Was it part of the plan for him never to come back, then? How could Mr. Elwood be sure of it?

It came to her like a horrible bolt of lightning. The

only way to be sure Thomas never told the truth was to do away with him! Elwood meant to *kill* Thomas! That was why he had sent him out of town with his trunk. He was going to lure him to some abandoned spot and murder him. And here she sat at a stupid rout party, wasting her time. She shot up from her seat and looked helplessly around the empty room. She must get home now, at once, and tell her aunt what she had figured out. She hurried toward the door and nearly capsized Mr. Delamar as he came in.

Chapter Three

"So here you are!" Mr. Delamar exclaimed. "I had begun to worry you'd gone haring off on some new mad scheme."

Surprise lent a sharp edge to her voice. "What are you doing here?"

"Looking for you. Your aunt told me where you'd gone."

"But how did you get in?"

A satirical smile lifted his brows. "I was invited, ma'am. Some people, you see, mistake me for a gentleman. Not all the ladies have your discernment."

She realized she'd been rude, and even regretted it, but the more important matter prevented her from wasting time on social niceties. "I have to go home at once."

"Your aunt had a much better idea. She suggested I act as your partner, to inform the world you were considering jilting Thomas."

"I have no intention of jilting Thomas! I must go home at once."

"I see you have some monumental new notion you want to share with your aunt. I am completely in her confidence. Tell me instead—while we dance. Just one dance. I promised Lady Lynne."

The beginning strains of a waltz filtered along the corridor. She looked at Mr. Delamar and saw such determination that she decided to humor him. He was an immensely determined young man, and if she could convince him of Thomas's innocence and of his danger, he would be a great help. Who better than a bloodhound to chase after that sly fox, Elwood, and bring him to justice? The *Harbinger* would later do an excellent job of explaining Thomas's innocence.

"Very well," she said, and put her hand on his arm. When they entered the ballroom, the hostess darted toward them. It was not Lady Faith she was honoring, but Mr. Delamar. "Guy, I was wondering where you'd got to! I was afraid you'd only come to jot down a few notes for your paper and run off again without dancing. I have half a dozen young ladies eager to meet you."

"All in good time, Mrs. Degrue. Lady Faith has promised me this waltz."

"Beware of him!" Mrs. Degrue smiled spitefully at Faith. "He will pick all your secrets out of your brain and publish them in his wicked paper. Such secrets as you have, too, Lady Faith! I look forward to reading about them." She went along, laughing, to the next couple.

Faith kept her tongue between her teeth, but the effort caused her to turn pink.

"Don't pay her any heed," Mr. Delamar said, and led her on to the floor.

"I don't waltz very well," Faith told him bluntly. "I was only given permission at Almack's to try it two weeks ago, and Thomas doesn't waltz."

He inclined his head and smiled. "Are you trying to confirm my opinion of Lord Thomas's poor sense? The waltz is the greatest thing to come along since damped gowns."

"And equally unhealthy," she said stiffly.

"Are you speaking of physical health, Lady Faith, or moral? I admit I was considering the damped gowns from an observer's point of view. For ladies, they are unhealthy in winter, but a waltz can do no harm in any season—to physical well-being, I mean."

Faith became aware that many people were watching them as they danced. She was no longer under any misapprehension that she was the one of interest. They were staring at Mr. Delamar, and not with disapproval.

"Well?" he asked. "Come now, I expect a counter-argument, Lady Faith. Surely you didn't call the waltz unhealthy without some substantiating evidence."

On those few occasions when she waltzed, Faith kept careful track of the count. One, two, three—one, two, three. She tried to think of a reply and lost track of the count, which caused her foot to come down rather hard on his. "There, you see, I told you it was dangerous," she exclaimed.

"No, you only said unhealthy. There is a difference; danger is more enjoyable. You must pardon my rattling on so nonsensically. What was it you wanted to say about Thomas?" He looked at her eyes, large with fear, and felt a quickening of interest.

"I think Mr. Elwood is going to murder him."

"What?"

It was surprising enough that he missed a beat and she landed on his foot again.

"It stands to reason. He only brought Thomas into his scheme to reach people who could buy the stocks and to make him the scapegoat when he ran off with the money." She explained her thinking in some detail, which played awful havoc with their waltz.

She expected an outright contradiction and was gratified when he heard her out thoughtfully, asking a few questions to draw her out. "It's not impossible," he admitted, "but in any case, I shouldn't think the deed has been done yet. Lord Thomas left alone this morning. I did some snooping around and learned that Elwood was seen at his office late this ev ng. He's miles behind Lord Thomas. That's why I went there for a look around. If you had cooperated with me this afternoon, we'd have Elwood under lock and key by now. Why didn't you tell me you knew where his office was?"

"Because you believed Thomas was guilty. How could I help you persecute him? He's my fiancé."

"I'm not persecuting anyone. I'm after the truth. That's

what makes the *Harbinger* rather special, if you can forgive my boasting a little. Well, the thing to do is to go after them.''

''Have you any idea where they've gone?''

''Only an idea, but also an idea where to discover more clues now that the evening traffic is quiet. We must go now. Who is your chaperone? I'll make your excuses.''

''Mrs. Coates came with me. I have to deliver her home.''

''Leave her your carriage. I'll take you to Berkeley Square.''

''There won't be any cabs in the street at this hour,'' she pointed out.

Again that satirical light burned in his eyes. ''I skimp on the necessities and allow myself the luxury of a carriage.''

With a memory of his miserable flat above the paper's office, she was by no means sure he could afford a carriage, and if he drove one, she hadn't seen it on Tottenham Court Road. ''I didn't see your carriage at Elwood's office.''

''I left if a block away. A good tip for you to follow next time you are illegally entering an establishment. I saw yours, which is why I was at pains not to enter by the front door and so alert your groom.''

''I'm not actually in the habit of entering establishments illegally. I doubt I shall use your tip.''

He refused to take offense. ''That would account for your mishandling of the situation,'' he said blandly. ''I'll speak to Mrs. Coates and get your wrap. Would you mind having a peek to see whose husband Lady Jersey has requisitioned this evening and what she's wearing? Mam'selle Ondit is doing her in the next issue. It's time she was repaid for her unconscionable rudeness to everyone.''

The triviality of this request, coming in the midst of more serious matters, was distasteful to Faith. Would Delamar really be of much help when half of his mind was on gossip? But she checked on these details for him and was able to report that Lady Jersey wore an unbecoming puce gown and stood up with Lord Castlereagh.

Mrs. DeGrue flew after Mr. Delamar when she saw him getting his coat. "You're not leaving already!" she complained. "Why, you just got here."

"Duty calls, ma'am. You must know the *Harbinger* has many parties to cover during this busy season, but I doubt I shall report any of the others to be such a stunning squeeze as yours."

Thus mollified, she let them go with no further pestering. As they went to the carriage, Faith felt some word of thanks was called for as Delamar was curtailing his regular business for her. "I daresay you would prefer to be going on to some ball or other instead of taking me home."

"The social scene is not my real interest. It's the hook to get ladies to buy the paper. Once it's on the sofa table, their husbands read the more interesting pieces. Originally, the *Harbinger* did a deal of such trivial stuff to encourage circulation, but it's shrunk to Mam'selle Ondit's column now."

"Still, it must require attendance at many parties to gather all Mam'selle's gossip."

"Mam'selle Ondit is composed of many people. I'm just her conscience. I decide what items to include. Her legs and eyes are several different ladies. Lady Marie Struthers is taking in the Ankers' ball for me tonight. She's an astute observer."

"Lady Marie! How did you meet her?" she asked in surprise.

He adopted a lazy smile and said, "Her chaperone fell asleep one evening and I, being a cur, naturally took advantage of the situation to foist myself on the young lady."

"There is no need to be satirical, Mr. Delamar."

"If you knew the alternative, you would not say so," he said through thinned lips.

Mr. Delamar's carriage, when it rolled up to the door,

32

was seen to be in the highest kick of fashion, and the team of bays harnessed to it were prime goers. But that Lady Marie Struthers was on close-enough terms to be reporting for him was the greater shock.

"How does it happen I never see you anywhere when apparently you attend a good many parties?" she asked.

"I must assume we don't often attend the same parties, though I've seen you a few times here and there. My more intimate friends are Whigs, you see, and it's well known the Mordains are high Tories."

"I see."

"Oh, I am not actually a partisan—objectivity is essential to good reporting—but I first established my reputation by doing some articles on the plight of returned veterans and it made me a minor hero with the Whigs."

"I thought your first reputation was based on social trivia," she reminded him.

"That doesn't establish a reputation, ma'am, only notoriety, which is, unfortunately, the easiest step for a man without connections. Hot gossip catches on more quickly than serious news."

"I wouldn't have thought you'd be interested in the easiest step."

"I was in a hurry. Poverty is a sharp goad, but you wouldn't know anything about that."

"I know something about being in a hurry at least. How long do you think it will take to find Thomas?"

He looked across the dark carriage to where she sat in the shadows. "We can cut an hour off the time if you'll agree to something a trifle unusual," he said diffidently.

"Of course, anything."

"You are precipitate—you didn't even ask what I had in mind."

"I would do anything for Thomas," she announced nobly.

Darkness concealed his disbelieving stare. "I'm going to make a reconnaissance mission to Lord Thomas's flat in Albany. It's practically on our way home. It wouldn't do for a lady to visit that bachelor establishment in the ordinary way, but you might be some help to me. I'm thinking of an address book with abbreviated names or places, a letter that would mean something to you but not to me. Are you game?"

"I'm not concerned with propriety when a man's life is at stake."

His eyes narrowed, though she couldn't see it in the dark carriage. "A man's life" seemed a vague, unemotional way for a lady to refer to her fiancé. "Especially when the man in question is the man you love," he said.

"Yes." Her answer was hardly more than a whisper.

The carriage drew up in a square cul-de-sac in front of a long, double row of houses. Thomas's flat was at the end nearer to Piccadilly. Mr. Delamar got out first and checked to see that no one was about. When he determined that the coast was clear, he gave Faith his hand, and together they ran to the door.

"How are we going to get in?" she asked.

"The same way I got into Elwood's office. With this." He held up a small metal tool, not a *passe-partout* key but a twisted piece of metal. The front door was unlocked, but he used it to open the door to Thomas's chambers. They stepped in to a pitch-black, airless room.

"There must be a lamp or some candles here somewhere," Faith whispered.

"We'll draw the draperies first."

When this was done, they found a lamp and lit it. The flat wore the disheveled look of a dwelling hastily abandoned. The desk in the corner stood with its drawers open, and papers were strewn about on top and on the floor. They went first to investigate these, but the papers were mostly bills, with a sprinkling of IOUs. Faith found a few letters but hesitated to read Thomas's private correspondence.

"What have you got there?" Delamar asked.

"It's from Thomas's father. I—I don't think we should read it."

Without an instant's hesitation, he reached for the letter. "My conscience is less scrupulous. I put a man's

34

life above his privacy." He glanced quickly through the two pages. "Nothing of interest to me here. It's about your marriage settlement." She looked at him with sharp interest. "Sure you don't want to take a peek? Just read it with one eye, the way Methodists dance on one leg," he tempted.

"No, thank you. I'll have a look in the bedroom."

"Intestinal fortitude as well as grace under pressure! You would have made a fine soldier."

Faith did not appear to be listening. She lit another lamp and went off alone to the bedchamber. It was in a mess, with the bed unmade and soiled shirts and cravats scattered about. The clothespress door was slightly ajar. On the bedside table rested a stack of gentlemen's magazines. They were of no weighty sort, mainly sporting and sartorial literature. Thomas had never posed as a heavy intellectual. She noticed the picture of herself was missing. That at least he had taken with him, which showed a continued regard for her. She went to the dresser and saw that the drawers were empty except for his Book of Common Prayer. She was saddened to see that he had left it behind; it almost seemed a symbol that he had abandoned proper thinking. It put the awful idea into her head that Thomas was indeed guilty. She was standing, holding the book in her hand and frowning, when Delamar appeared at the door. He went to the wardrobe and flung the door open. A diaphanous red peignoir hung haphazardly on a hanger.

Faith turned and saw Mr. Delamar running his hands over it. He looked at her, one eyebrow cocked at a quizzing angle.

She stared, unbelieving, at the peignoir, but her first instinct was to protect Thomas. "His sister sometimes visits," she said curtly.

"I admire her taste, though I shouldn't like to see such an item on my own sister if I had one. And neither would Lord Thomas."

Her hand longed to reach out and slap his bold face. It took all her willpower to restrain it. But really it was Thomas she wanted to revile. How could he? Of course

35

she knew Thomas was a flirt—all the women were after him. That peignoir had probably hung in the closet for months, untouched—since long before their engagement.

"Take it, then, if you admire it, Mr. Delamar. Thomas is through with it and its owner, I assure you," she said with a semblance of calm.

He shook his head and a reluctant smile broke out. "Propriety wins out—again. One day that composure will break and London will suffer another earthquake."

"Not at all. There is nothing unusual in a bachelor's entertaining a woman in his rooms."

He shrugged his shoulders. "I've got what I'm after. Let's go. Or have you found something?" he asked, looking at the book in her hands.

"No, just a book," she said, and closed the drawer. "What did you find?"

"We'll discuss it in the carriage. We don't want to loiter here longer than necessary. Douse the lamp."

Delamar held his ear to the door before leaving. They hurried down the stairs and out to the waiting carriage.

"What did you find?" she asked.

"A map. I already knew he'd been to a travel agent and was inquiring for ships abroad. Now I know what port he's headed for and what ship he's booked passage on."

"Dover?"

"No, the surprising thing is that he's marked Bournemouth. Not the fastest route to France. You don't suppose he's making a dart to America? His agent implied he was going to France."

"Thomas—America?" she asked, astonished. "I shouldn't think so. I can't see Thomas with dusty boots and provincial society. He's a town buck. It must be Elwood's doing. He's luring Thomas to Bournemouth to kill him there, in that out-of-the-way spot, where no one will recognize him. I mean, no one goes to Bournemouth."

"Does his family own any real estate on the Isle of Wight?"

"No. This is Elwood's idea, I tell you," she said impatiently. "Will you go after him?"

"I'll be leaving tonight as soon as I deliver you home."

"He's innocent, you know," she said softly. "You must believe that." And she must believe it, too. She must have faith in Thomas. If nothing else, the fact that he was cut off from England and all of his friends would prevent him from acting so badly. "Promise me you won't do anything to hurt him."

Delamar's voice, when he answered, was cutting. "I am not an assassin. I don't shoot first and ask questions after."

"I was thinking of your being a soldier. Killing would be nothing new for you."

"The war is over. I'm a journalist now, not a professional killer."

When the carriage pulled up to Lady Lynne's house, Delamar opened the door and accompanied Faith inside to speak to her aunt.

"Ah, good. You found her and brought her home. How did the rout party go, Faith?" Lady Lynne asked. "Did you tell the old cats what I told you to?"

"Yes."

"Did anyone dance with you?"

"I stood up a few times."

"I made her waltz, as I promised," Mr. Delamar added.

"Poor you!" Lady Lynne laughed. "Faith has two left feet when it comes to waltzing, but she will soon get the hang of it."

"She's as supple as a cat already. She always landed on *my* feet," he said, and smiled at Faith to show her that he was joking.

"What's that you've got there, Guy?" was the chaperone's next question.

Faith looked surprised to hear her aunt on such familiar terms with Mr. Delamar after so short an acquaintance. He placed the map on the table, and they all gathered around to look at it.

"He has this line drawn between London and Bournemouth," Delamar said, tracing the route with his finger. "He's going by way of Winchester—he wouldn't get that far today. Lady Faith thinks it's France he'd be headed for. What do you think, Lady Lynne?"

"Thomas would like Paris, but don't folks usually go by the shortest route, from Dover to Calais?"

"Yes, but if he's on the run, he wouldn't go the usual way and Bournemouth is not far from Cherbourg," Delamar explained. "These notes Lord Thomas made indicate that America is his destination. On the other hand, he might have left the map and notes behind to throw dust in our eyes. There's a ship to America leaving Bournemouth later this week. Is he that cunning, in your estimation?"

"Thomas is not cunning, and he is not a thief," Faith said firmly. "Elwood arranged the whole thing. I think he means to murder Thomas, Auntie."

"Rubbish!" was her aunt's opinion of that. "Murder is a very serious matter. He'd stick at murder. No, he may very well have conned Thomas into dashing off to Bournemouth on some pretext or other. His aim may have been to set the law chasing after Thomas while he slipped away somewhere else with our money. Otherwise they would have gone off together, I think. Do you have any line on Elwood at all, Guy?"

"He was spotted leaving his office this evening. Unfortunately, the man who saw him didn't follow him, so I have no way of knowing where he was going. I only learned tonight where his office was or I'd have had it watched, of course."

"Why, we knew all along! You should have asked us!"

"I *did* ask you for your help, ma'am," he reminded her, but it was Faith who was subjected to an accusing glare.

"Then you shall have it," Lady Lynne said, and laughed. "We shall accompany you on this mad dash to Bournemouth. It will get Faith out of town, away from all of the old cats who are sharpening their claws to rip her to ribbons.''

"I travel alone," Delamar said simply.

"Fine, then we'll travel along beside you."

"That is a bad idea. There might be trouble. It's no place for ladies," Delamar said through thinned lips.

"The highways are common property," Lady Lynne riposted.

Faith quickly considered this outlandish idea and found much to recommend it. Getting away from the cats of London was as tempting as helping to prove Thomas innocent. "I have every right to go, more right than you," she told Delamar.

His face took on a forbidding aspect. "I can't stop you, but don't expect me to slow down to ten miles an hour to accommodate you."

Lady Lynne tossed her head. "My late husband had the best bits of blood money can buy, and I have them still. Ten miles an hour, indeed! Call for the carriage, Faith. The traveling carriage. Oh, bother, my groom is at the Degrues' rout. I'll send a footman after him while we throw a few things into cases."

Then there was the great commotion of Delamar stalking out of the house, of a footman rushing after the groom, of servants assisting with the packing, and of a few social engagements that had to be canceled at the last minute.

It was while Faith folded linens into a valise that she began to wonder why Mr. Delamar was going after Thomas when she knew in her bones that it was Elwood who was the guiltier party. Of course they didn't know where Elwood had gone, while Thomas, being less cunning, had left a trail. Still, with all his connections, Mr. Delamar ought to be able to snoop out something, or how had he earned his reputation as a bloodhound? For her part, she was sure Elwood was following Thomas to kill him, and she wondered if Mr. Delamar believed it as well. It added to her nervousness that he might believe it. His disbelief had given her hope that it was untrue.

39

Some small corner of her mind had begun to put faith in his intelligence, if nothing else. And if it was true, they must make haste to overtake Elwood before he murdered Thomas.

Chapter Four

It was more than an hour later by the time Lady Lynne's traveling carriage was packed and ready for the journey. Any person with a ha'pence of common sense knew that it was ridiculous to strike out into the night on such an uncertain quest, but Faith did not say so, in case her aunt changed her mind.

Lady Lynne made herself comfortable on a pile of pillows and said, "I mean to catch a few winks, my dear. If Guy's carriage is spotted, awaken me. Or, better still, have Nubbins whip up the team and keep it in sight."

"I imagine he's miles ahead of us already, Auntie."

"I had hoped he'd offer to take us in his carriage. That would have been more . . . interesting. But then it's as well to have two rigs," the aunt said, and then said no more. The soft, lascivious smile that curved her lips was concealed by the shadows. In her mind's eye, it was only she and Guy who dashed through the night in his carriage while Faith remained here in comfortable isolation. It wouldn't do to have that Bath miss witnessing things she shouldn't.

Lady Lynne was quite charmed by her daring in going after Lord Thomas. The idea had come to her during Guy's visit to Berkeley Square, when he had seemed most amenable to flirtation. She hadn't had a lover since Sir John's death. Long deprivation had heightened her desire and limited her common sense. But Guy Delamar had been worth every second of the wait. How society would stare to learn that the elusive journalist had fallen into her lap. Mind you, he would not be easy to manage, but she had no taste for easy tasks.

The dame was soon snoring lightly. Faith pulled a blanket over her shoulders and gazed out the window at the passing show of London, soon petering out to countryside with intermittent splotches of housing developments. She looked but saw none of the scenery. Her mind was back at Thomas's flat, imagining him there with a lightskirt in a red peignoir. The thought caused a heavy ache in her heart. She knew his reputation and had felt proud that she was the one he had chosen to cure him of that propensity, but had she cured him? What if he had been seeing a woman even after their engagement? At the very least, it indicated some lack in his scruples not to have thrown out the peignoir. Any of his friends might have seen it there.

Ahead, the first tollbooth loomed and the driver slowed down. Instead of cracking the whip and picking up speed after he had paid the toll, he drew to another stop. Faith opened the door to see what was delaying him and saw a man approaching. Her first rush of fear that it was a highwayman subsided when she recalled that they were still close to London.

Even before the man was close enough to see his face, she recognized the swaggering walk and broad shoulders of Mr. Delamar.

"So you really came!" he exclaimed curtly. "I made sure the practical Lady Faith would dissuade her aunt from such folly."

"As you see, we are here. I thought you would be much farther along the road by now."

"I had some business to attend to before leaving town. If you're really going to Bournemouth, it will be better for us to travel close together. The scamps are less likely to hold up a pair of carriages."

"Highwaymen, you mean?" she asked nervously.

"Yes. I hope you ladies aren't carrying any jewelry."

"I don't know what my aunt may have packed. I have

42

only this," she said, and lifted her hand to display her engagement ring. It was a narrow band encircled with baguette diamonds.

Mr. Delamar glanced at it dismissingly. "I shouldn't think that would attract Jeb Throwe's interest. He is the scamp who works this stretch of road. We are on terms, Jeb and I. Don't be frightened if he comes pelting out of the shadows firing his pistol into the air. He's really not such a bad fellow. I'll tell him you're with me."

She gave him a disparaging glare. "How convenient for you, to be on terms with all the local criminals, Mr. Delamar."

"Equally convenient for *you* to be on terms with *me*, Lady Faith. Don't bite the hand that protects you." He turned on his heel and went back to his carriage.

"Keep close behind his carriage," Faith called to Nubbins, and closed the door.

She was soon subjected to a merciless jostling. She was convinced Mr. Delamar set this ridiculous pace on purpose to aggravate her, but she refused to be angry. Speed was what suited her purpose, and she didn't mind the jostling. She followed her aunt's lead and tried to settle in to rest, but there was no rest for her, though Lady Lynne was dozing quietly. Faith was still half awake much later when Nubbins stopped to change the team. She saw Mr. Delamar get out of his carriage and thought he might come to have a word with her, but he only spoke to the ostler and returned to his own carriage.

The next time she opened her eyes, the black shadows of night had dissipated and an orange ball of fire lit the skies. The carriage stood in front of a half-timbered inn from whose front door Mr. Delamar suddenly issued. He saw her face at the carriage window and came toward her. He looked perfectly refreshed, clean-shaven, and wore fresh linens, while she was cramped and wrinkled, and hungry. He had let them sit sleeping while he ate breakfast and changed! Already out of spirits because of Thomas, it was enough to cause a surge of vexation to well up in her. She opened the door and climbed out.

43

"You might have at least let us know we were stopped!" she charged in a voice suited to rebuking servants. "How long have we wasted sleeping while you prepared yourself for the next lap?"

Sunlight beamed on his face, causing him to narrow his eyes, but she read the anger in those twin slits. He slowly drew out his watch and studied it. "Five minutes. I have ordered breakfast. Please hurry. I don't want to waste any more time than necessary. I'll be leaving within the hour." He turned abruptly and strode off toward the stable.

Faith woke her aunt from a sound sleep, and together they went into the inn. Lady Lynne went to the desk and said pompously, "We require a room immediately. We shan't be staying; we only want to freshen up before taking breakfast. You must hurry, as we are in a rush."

The innkeeper shook his head. "We're all booked up, m'lady. There's a great boxing match on here today, you must know. Tom Cribb is taking on Lefty Legree, Lord Henderson's boy, trained by Jackson. We haven't so much as an inglenook to offer you."

"You found a room for Mr. Delamar!" Faith said petulantly.

"Guy Delamar . . . are *you* the ladies he spoke to me about?" the innkeeper asked. His expression changed to one of warm amiability. "In that case, just step along here behind me. It's my own room he used, and you're welcome to it as well. I've had hot water and clean towels taken up. You'll be wanting your things from the carriage, I figure? But you must step lively, ladies. The private parlor Guy arranged belongs by rights to another gentleman. I happen to know Mr. Severn won't be down for a bit yet as he was celebrating till nearly morning. Right this way." He walked off, with the ladies trailing behind him. They were soon in the innkeeper's bedchamber, and their valises were brought up.

"This was thoughtful of Guy," Lady Lynne said. "I wonder what it cost him?"

"Whatever it is, we must repay him," Faith replied.

44

"Pay him?" Lady Lynne laughed. "My dear, you daren't offer money to the likes of Delamar. Those boys on the fringe of gentility are as easily wounded as maidens. But we shall thank him very graciously, of course."

"Boy" seemed to Faith a poor description of Mr. Delamar. She was annoyed by so many things she hardly knew what was bothering her. Having called him to account unjustly was a part of it, of course. The awareness that she must apologize rankled, and her aunt's cavalier manner of accepting favors added to her chagrin. Perhaps most vexing of all was that he could obtain services with apparent ease when they had been denied to her aunt and herself.

"I expect he had to come down handsomely to get a room at such a busy time," Faith mentioned.

"Perhaps not. It might be a matter of barter—a mention of this inn in the *Harbinger* would be worth something. That's how clever men do business, my girl."

They hurried their toilette and were soon downstairs being shown into Mr. Severn's private parlor. Lady Lynne looked around the empty room. "Is Guy not joining us, I wonder?" she asked.

The same thought had occurred to Faith. "I notice three places are set. What can be keeping him?"

The waiter poured coffee and went to get their food. By the time it arrived, Mr. Delamar was back. "Good morning, ladies. I hope you haven't waited for me. I've been making inquiries in the stables for Lord Thomas. No one here has seen him."

Lady Lynne threw him a coquettish smile and poured his coffee. "You have arranged our stop very well, Guy. The innkeeper was ready to show us the door till Faith inadvertently dropped your name."

"There's a boxing match today, which is why they're so busy," he explained. "I'd give my left arm to see it."

Faith had offered no thanks, so to add a helpful word at least she said, "Would it be possible to have one of the gentlemen staying here cover the story for the *Harbinger*?"

"My sports writer is here. It wasn't the reporting I referred to. I'd like to see it for my own enjoyment."

"I swear all men are animals at heart," Lady Lynne exclaimed, and shook her head at the tiger who graced her table. "But then you were a soldier, Guy, and no doubt miss the fun of shooting and looting, eh?"

Lady Lynne was about as sensitive as a chair, but her niece noticed the darkening flush that crept up from Mr. Delamar's collar and the quick quivering of a muscle in his jaw before he answered. "I find plenty of violence in England to fill the void, ma'am."

"I bet you do!" Lady Lynne said, and laughed merrily. "Though the footpads are not so bad as they used to be. We called twilight the Footpad Hour, a few years back. When I was just a girl," she added hastily.

"I wasn't referring to criminal violence in particular," Mr. Delamar said. "The greater and more lamentable violence is perfectly legal and is directed against the poor. The Luddites were treated as criminals when they tried to present their case to the Parliamentary Committee on the Woolen Trade. We have children scarcely weaned working from dawn to dark in factories and mines; farmers being ruined by enclosure; a system of voting that robs the poor of any say in the making of laws; and a monarchy who considers its prime function is to waste money while thousands starve. I find plenty of violence to keep me amused," he said grimly.

"But what a good show Prinney and his brothers put on for us all. I swear it is almost worth whatever huge sum they cost us. They're better than Covent Garden. You'll get nowhere with that radical kind of talk, sir," Lady Lynne cautioned him. "If you want to make your way in England, you must turn Tory. Why, I was just telling my niece the other day, titles grow like weeds on Fleet Street. If you espoused the proper causes in your paper, you might find yourself wearing a handle one of these days. How would you like that?"

"I *do* espouse the proper causes. I expect you mean the *popular* ones. Let the *Morning Post* and the *Morning Her-*

ald praise the vice of the Tories. I personally consider a title little better than an insult. Look into their history and you'll almost invariably find that titles were conferred for some extraordinary act of servility or criminality to their monarch on the part of the nobleman concerned. In the case of the ladies, becoming a king's mistress is usually the preferred route. Present company excepted, of course," he added as a sop when he saw Faith's eyes begin to shoot sparks.

"Sour grapes." Lady Lynne laughed.

"Sour thoughts but true," he replied, and lifted his fork.

"I cannot let that pass unchallenged," Faith declared. "Most of the titles were conferred for outstanding bravery in battle—in France, and at Culloden, and . . ." History was not her long suit.

Delamar lifted a mobile brow. His eyes were trained on her like pistols. "I grant you there were a few brave gentlemen rewarded for their heroics in days long past. Marlborough comes to mind. How does that entitle their families for countless generations to consider themselves in any way special?"

"We share consanguinity!" she shot back. "The blood of those same heroes flows in our veins, uninterrupted over the centuries."

"Except for an occasional adulterine child foisted on an unsuspecting father. You forget the corroding influence of time as well. Nothing lasts forever, including brave blood. The House of Lords has thrown up more congenital idiots than can be found in Bedlam," he said baldly.

"Do you object to the titles bestowed on Wellington?" Faith asked.

"You have chosen an odd example! He earned them at the risk of his life, unlike the raft of peers created for no reason but to stack the house and get a bill through the Lords. What I object to is that centuries after a hero's death, when power has corrupted the line, the family can still trade on his past glories. I believe titles ought not to be hereditary. But I didn't mean to mount my hobbyhorse,"

47

he added more mildly. "No doubt there are some fine hereditary lords, as there are fine carpenters and scholars and butchers."

"Let us agree to disagree, and have done with it," Faith said dampingly. "You found no trace of Thomas, you say. Did you inquire for Mr. Elwood?"

"Naturally. There are dozens of inns on this road. They stopped elsewhere, that's all. We'll forge on to Bournemouth. Unless you ladies have reconsidered and want to return to London?" he asked hopefully.

"You do think Elwood is following Thomas, then?" Faith asked.

He gave her a long, hard look. "Perhaps he's chasing him," he said.

It was the first time this possibility had been introduced, and as it escalated Thomas to the prime suspect, Faith bristled up in his defense. "I assure you that is not the case."

"My queries in London told me it was Thomas who kept the blunt. It was banked in his name. He withdrew the lot just before he took off. Elwood left later. Logic suggests he's following the blunt. Still want to continue with the hunt?"

Reason fled and a red anger engulfed her. "So that's why you aren't interested in Elwood! You think Thomas robbed *him* as well as the investors. You certainly don't know much about him. Thomas is a gentleman, sir. Gentlemen do not behave so, though one can understand *your* not being aware of it." His shoulders stiffened, but she no longer felt guilty at slighting his origins.

"True, I wasn't born at the top of the hill, which accounts for my more realistic estimation of how a gentleman will behave, when he is goaded."

"Thomas was not goaded."

"He was expected to marry you!" he shot back fiercely.

Faith took a breath, preparing herself to rise and stalk from the room. Her aunt read the signs and placed a restraining hand on her arm. "Children, children! Such argument is very bad for the digestion. Do try some of this

48

lovely plum preserve, Guy." He sat like a lead soldier while she placed a blob of the preserve on his plate. "I cannot imagine why we are arguing about titles and gentlemen and commoners. It has nothing to do with our problem. As far as that goes, I am no more than genteel myself. I was born Miss Haversham, you know, Faith, and Sir John was as common as dirt. He was knighted for finally getting elected a Tory, and that is all that allows me to be called Lady Lynne."

"I am not ashamed of living by my wits," Guy said as a peace offering.

It was spurned out of hand. "That would account for the paucity of your living accommodations," Faith said angrily.

Her aunt felt a pronounced desire to shake the girl. As this was ineligible, she decided to give her a more subtle lesson. "As to the Mordain title," she said spitefully, "you hit the nail on the head, Guy. One of Faith's female ancestors had the wits to oblige her monarch, and he conferred the earldom on her husband."

"The first Lord Mordain was an officer in the king's army!" Faith said.

"That is true, my dear. The king wished him away and sent him off to France."

Delamar looked down his nose at Faith and remarked blandly, "*Now* you will accept my opinion that time dilutes the blood."

She glared at him but refused to acknowledge the hit. "Shall we go now, Auntie? As soon as we have paid for our share of this stop, of course."

Her aunt smiled appeasingly at Guy, then turned to her troublesome niece. "Run along and have our valises brought down, dear, while we settle up here."

The settling up consisted of no more than a polite thank-you and an apology for her niece's farouche behavior. To explain it away, she added, "The poor child is pushed beyond reason by this business. She is so desperately in love with Thomas, you must know."

He regarded her critically. "Yesterday you called it

49

fondness. This accretion of love is sudden, *n'est-ce-pas*?''

Lady Lynne's real interest was to note that Guy was capable of a French phrase, and in a good accent, too, but as some reply needed to be made, she said, ''It was rather more than that, as it turns out. She is a private sort of person and keeps her feelings to herself.''

''She doesn't keep her dislike under such close wraps.''

''You were rather hard on her, I think. The family name means so much to her. Glory is all that survives, really. The money has been gone for decades.''

''As I understand it, Lord Thomas wasn't well to grass, either. What did they propose to live on?''

''Love—and a pittance. Unwise, but then she is young. She had an excellent offer from Mr. Morrison, a fellow whose papa runs a brewery, but blue blood and beer do not mix. She preferred Lord Thomas's poverty.''

''*Chacun à son goût,*'' he said, and shrugged his shoulders.

''You did not pick up that French accent in Spain, Guy. Wherever did you learn it?''

He gave a derisive smile and said, ''In the gutters of Paris. Travel is broadening, they say. It ought to be on the curriculum of ladies' seminaries; it might yank the chits out of their ignorant self-complacency.''

''It did not sound like gutter French to me, but then I am as ignorant as a swan. I have never been abroad and lay no claim to any decent education whatsoever. What I know, I learned from novels.''

''It is refreshing to hear a lady admit the truth. You have developed at least an understanding of human nature,'' he said, and held the door for her.

The two carriages were soon rattling along the road toward Bournemouth. Lady Lynne decided to take her niece to task in hopes of more harmonious stops in the future.

''It was not necessary for you to display your provincial upbringing for Mr. Delamar's benefit, Faith,'' she said sternly. ''If you have any hope of finding Thomas, you'd better humor the fellow. You and I wouldn't have much chance without him. He had a few things to say about your ignorance."

"I have no interest in Mr. Delamar's opinion of me," she asserted comprehensively, then looked from the corner of her eyes to hear the details.

"Personal comments are always in poor taste. We'll have no more jibes at his impoverished background. I begin to think he was not so deprived as I had thought. He speaks very good French at least."

"He is the one who started it by running down the aristocracy."

"There's something to be said for his views, but that is strictly *entre nous*. In public one must pretend to admire tired old blood or you'd never be invited anywhere. It is a pity Guy is so Whiggish. On the other hand, the Whig aristocrats are much more amusing and stylish. I wonder if he has the entrée to polite Whig saloons."

"Lady Marie Struthers does some reporting for him," Faith mentioned.

"Marie Struthers! You don't mean it! Why, she is top of the trees. I daresay he hopes to nab her and establish himself in society." This was hard news, indeed. Lady Lynne was astute enough to realize her own worn charms would be hopeless against such stiff competition as the incomparable Lady Marie.

Before they had gone a mile, she had hatched a new scheme. If it was an unexceptional bride Mr. Delamar was after, he might replace Lord Thomas. She *did* hate to ruin her record for making matches, and upon hearing that Thomas had been the banker for the stolen funds, she assumed him to be guilty. She slid a sly eye at her niece and said, "I slept very poorly last night, Faith. When we stop to change horses, I wonder if you'd mind removing to Guy's carriage for one stage. It will give me a chance to put my feet up on the other seat and catch a few winks."

"I'd sooner walk all the way in tight shoes."

This was entirely the correct response. Lady Lynne was perfectly aware of the antagonism between them and welcomed it. There was nothing so stimulating to the blood as hot argument. How she and John used to battle—and how they made up afterward!

"Walk, then, by all means," she said, "unless you'd prefer to sit up on the driver's bench with Nubbins, for I mean to put you out of my bedchamber."

Chapter Five

Lady Lynne made good her threat. When the two carriages stopped at Horsham to change teams and allow the passengers to refresh themselves, she sent her niece off to buy newspapers while she got Delamar aside and asked him if he would mind having company in his rig. The mischievous sparkle in her eye filled him with foreboding as to her intentions of attaching him, for she had been gay almost to giddiness over lunch to cover up Faith's silence.

"I would be a poor traveling companion," he said. "I am writing as we go along. The rag still has to be got out, you know, even if I am not sitting behind my desk."

The sparkle in her eye turned to steely determination. "Surely you do not require two banquettes to do your writing?"

"I do my best writing when I am alone. Such a charming companion as yourself, Lady Lynne, would distract me no end."

She smiled at this graceful put-off and then revealed his error. "If you are that easily distracted, sir, then there is no point in telling you it is my niece who wished to share your coach. It goes without saying her charms exceed my own."

She noticed the leap of interest in his eyes and the dismay that he had misjudged the situation. In different circumstances, she would have let him stew, but time was limited, so she went on to clinch the matter. "Well, it is mighty uncivil of you, Guy," she said jokingly. "I am so fatigued with the jostling that I thought I might catch a few winks if I could get my carriage to myself, but your work must take precedence, of course."

"Never let it be said I robbed a lady of her beauty sleep. I shouldn't think Lady Faith will overburden me with chatter. Is she generally so untalkative?"

"Not usually, but you need not fear she'll prose your ear off today. Ah, here she is now!" she exclaimed as Faith returned to the parlor with the newspaper. "You are to go the next lap in Guy's carriage, my dear. It is all arranged. And you must not pester him with conversation as he is in the throes of writing for his paper." Then she put her hand on Faith's arm and led her out before she could publicly vent her objections.

Even before the carriage left the inn yard, Faith opened the paper and began to read it. Indeed she had brought it along for no other reason than to inhibit conversation if her aunt insisted on making her ride with Mr. Delamar. It was the Tory *Times* that she held in front of her. Being much less sly than her aunt, she intended no slur in this choice but only bought the paper her father always had in the house. The only sound within as the carriage drove through the little market town was the scratching of pencil on pad and the rustling of the newspaper. Faith glanced at an old church with perpendicular windows and a shingle spire but found it not worth a comment. At West Horsham, Mr. Delamar lifted his head to observe the redbrick buildings of St. Martin's Hospital. Not a word had been exchanged between them thus far.

"That is St. Martin's Hospital," he mentioned.

She lowered the paper an inch and peered over the top of it. "Oh, yes."

Before she could raise her paper again, he pointed out a group of schoolboys in the yard. "They look like birds in their blue gowns and yellow stockings. We may be staring at a future prime minister or judge or murderer, depending in large part on what sort of school it is."

"I thought it was a hospital," she said.

"No, it is a Blue-Coat school, *called* St. Martin's Hospital, as Christ Church is a school called a church. There are historical reasons for the names, but I believe they continue the misnomers to confuse the hapless victims."

She let the paper settle on her knees. "Did you not care for school, Mr. Delamar? I enjoyed it tremendously."

"They don't make you ladies burst your heads learning Latin and Greek."

"No, we learn useful things like embroidery and poetry," she replied, taking note of his classical education. She condescended, in the interest of civility, to smile.

Thus encouraged, he decided she was tame enough to take a joke. "I notice you're reading the Thunderer. That will do you about as much good as your embroidery if it's information you're seeking. It earned its nickname by assuming the Olympian prerogative of oracular wisdom, couching its editorials in the royal 'we,' as though it were anything more than the Tory opinions of John Walter II."

"What does your paper's name signify, Mr. Delamar?"

"A harbinger is a forerunner, one who—and by extension which—announces coming events, as birds and blossoms are harbingers of spring. You will recall my favored position in any endeavor is the forefront. I try, in my paper, to point out what will occur if certain courses are followed."

She lifted a brow and pinned him with her brilliant eyes. "That would be *Tory* courses?" she asked.

"They've been the party in power for as long as I can remember, catering to the wishes of the aristocracy, the landed gentry, the church, and the established order in general."

"And are you against established tradition?"

"No, I am against prejudice, particularly when it disguises itself as right and reason. Even our courts, you know, allow every man's case to be heard. If we permit criminals that right, surely the innocent are due the same. I try to speak for those who are mute due to their lack of a forum. Someone ought to express outrage at such goings-on as the Prince of Wales being paid six hundred and thirty thousand pounds for marrying his German wife, who is a disgrace to the nation; his Oriental fantasy at Brighton costing nearly as much as the Peninsular War; and such details. But I know what side you are on, so I shan't carp.''

''I hope I am not on the side of ignorance and prejudice,'' she said defensively.

''If you at least *hope*, then you're not past cure and help, according to Mr. Shakespeare—one of my idols. I treasure him for his insights. Hope, however, is only an inanimate virtue till it inspires you to action. The action I am suggesting, in this roundabout way, is that you try reading my journal.''

With a charming smile, he handed her the latest copy of the *Harbinger*. ''I never waste an opportunity to gain a subscriber, you see. When I'm not writing, I'm promoting.''

She accepted the paper and then turned aside to catch the light over her shoulder, for the day was overcast. ''It is writing you should be doing now, so I'll read this and let you get back to work.''

''I look forward to hearing your opinion.''

She turned immediately to Mam'selle Ondit's column and read again his article on Thomas, which undid any good effect of their talk. He watched her quietly for a moment. His expression was gentle, even yearning, as his eyes flickered over her bent head and her profile. As time passed, he resumed his writing and she read other articles. She soon found herself adrift in a strange, new, and horrible world. He wrote stories—surely they were just stories, and not true—of whole families in the North and Midlands subjected to terrible deprivation. Husband, wife, and children all toiled long hours in factories or foundries under appalling conditions for a pittance. It seemed the greed of the mill and foundry owners was only half of the problem. The other half involved the corn laws, known to her thus far solely from her father's conversation and considered an excellent thing. But in the case of the poor, who had to buy rather than sell, these laws had the effect of raising the price of bread to some astronomical height. She became first interested, then outraged that such a thing could be. England, lately subject to poor harvests, had raised the price of grains; and to prevent people from buying imported grains at a lower price, the government imposed high import tariffs. How was it possible that the politicians, supported by her own father, allowed this dreadful thing to happen? Nay, encouraged it!

Mr. Delamar stole quiet glances at her from time to time as she read. He saw first her frowns of misunderstanding or disbelief and watched as anger gathered on her brow. He sat ready to expatiate further on political matters, but she had no intention of revealing the extent of her ignorance, so when she had finished reading, she just set the paper aside and looked out the window.

He put away his pencil and said, "We're in for a storm, to judge by that lead sky."

"Yes. The roads will be a regular hasty pudding. How far are we from Bournemouth?"

"We're coming to Amberley. This is the Arun River. There's a charming old ruined castle and a Norman church, but we shan't have time to view them today."

"Are we near Winchester yet?" she asked.

He handed her Thomas's folded map, and she studied it. "Amberley! Mr. Delamar, we're going the wrong way. Thomas marked Winchester on his map."

"We couldn't expect to overtake him at Winchester. We'll catch him at Bournemouth. That's where he sails from, tomorrow evening at nine. We're just taking a slightly different route. We'll go south, then west, instead of south-west. We'll have to ferry across the inlet, but it's no farther."

"I must have misunderstood the Pythagorean theorem! How can two sides of a triangle not be longer than the other one?"

"Not much longer," he said.

"Ferrying the carriages will be very awkward. Why aren't we going by Winchester?"

"I have to make a stop at Fareham. I have some business to attend to there."

"Did you learn something about Thomas?" she asked swiftly.

"No, it's another matter entirely."

"But that will waste time! We want to catch him as soon as possible. That's the only reason my aunt and I came."

A mask of arrogant indifference settled over his harsh features. "Lord Thomas is a minor matter as far as I'm concerned. *I* must stop at Fareham. Naturally you and your aunt are free to do as you wish. There is no fear of highwaymen in this part of the country. Their little vice near the coast is smuggling, not robbery."

She stared, incredulous. "You mean you aren't making this trip to follow Thomas?"

"Not *just* to catch him," he replied. He didn't emphasize "catch," but she noticed it and knew a man whose tools were words had not made the change by chance. He spoke on calmly, but calmness was at an end for Faith. Her companion was a clear and obvious enemy again. "There's a by-election at Fareham today. I have a man down there following the outcome. I have to see him."

"How long will you stop?" she asked stiffly.

"For as long as my business takes, but it need not detain *you*. *You* must continue your pursuit of Lord Thomas, by all means."

After that brusque exchange, they continued through the chalky South Downs. Castles and churches were observed in stony silence. As they drew nearer to the coast, the skies grew darker and a fierce wind carried the tangy sea scent in its grip. No rain had fallen yet, and the dry dust flew in clouds, while the tree branches whipped like sheets in the wind. Soon the ominous roll of thunder was heard reverberating in the heavens.

"Aunt Lynne will be frightened to death," Faith said. "Are we nearly at Fareham?"

"It won't be long now. With luck, we'll be there before the storm breaks." He sounded not only unconcerned but rather satisfied. It occurred to Faith that she and her aunt could hardly proceed on their quest in the teeth of a roaring storm. She was already irritated at the prospect of the ferry

58

crossing and had no intention of attempting it in bad weather.

When they reached Fareham, they found the little seaport to be bustling with activity, as voters made their way to and fro to cast their ballots. They drove to the Red Lion and waited a moment for Lady Lynne. Her carriage had remained close behind them all afternoon, but when they drew into the inn yard, there was no sign of it. "I hope my aunt hasn't had an accident," Faith said.

"Come along inside before the rain starts. I'll send my driver back for her." Delamar spoke to his groom and took her arm to propel her into the hostelry. It was a quaint, unsophisticated country inn with humble furnishings, but on this election day it was busy. "Do you think this storm is going to blow over soon?" he asked the proprietor.

"We're in for a gale it looks like," he was told. "You and your lady are lucky. I only have the one room left, and not my finest either, but you won't want to carry on your trip in this weather." He lifted a key and handed it to Guy. "The Mermaid Room is what I have available, sir."

Faith felt a moment's embarrassment at the misunderstanding, but there was no archness in Delamar's manner. "You and your aunt had best take it before it's gone," he advised her.

"But where will *you* sleep?"

"Don't worry about me. Unnecessary advice, I think?" he asked, slanting a mocking smile at her. She was loath to take the last room after his jibe. "Go ahead," he urged. "Your aunt won't thank you for offering to sleep on a bolster by the fireside. That's a gentleman's prerogative— I'll pretend I'm a gentleman, for tonight."

While she signed the register, he continued talking to the proprietor. "Is Dick Fletcher staying here?"

"Aye, we have Mr. Fletcher with us. You're in the shipping business as well, are you?"

"That's right," he lied, for there were occasions when a journalist did not advertise his true calling in the interest of hearing the truth. "Would you have any idea where I might find Mr. Fletcher?"

"He just stepped into the taproom for a wet. A roaring business we're doing today. We're having a by-election here, you must know. Old George Shaft, the Tory incumbent, has stuck his fork in the wall and his son is up to replace him."

"Is that so? I noticed the streets were busy. Who do you think will take it?"

"There's no question hereabouts. We always get stuck with a Tory. We'll get the Shaft again, I wager," he joked.

"I thought since the new Duke of Graveston took over, there might be some hope of a change," Guy said, to let his listener know his own sentiments.

"They do say the young duke is of a different stripe than his late papa, but the old gaffers have the scrutineering under their care, you see. No matter what goes into the box, what will come out of it is Mr. Shaft."

Delamar adopted a sympathetic face. "Like that, is it? Who's in charge of counting the vote here?"

"Shaft's man, a Mr. Irons by name—and an ironmonger by trade—but his avocation is feeding from the Tory trough. He always gets any sort of political job that can be done by an idiot—except that of Member of Parliament, of course," the proprietor added with a wink. "That plum belongs to Mr. Shaft."

Delamar arranged to have Faith taken to her room, and before she had removed her bonnet and pelisse, her aunt came in, shaking raindrops from her pelisse and complaining about the weather.

"You never saw such black clouds. It looks as though the heavens are in mourning. And the thunder! Loud enough to wake the dead. I barely got in before the clouds opened. Where is Guy?"

"He is looking up one of his employees in the taproom," Faith answered brusquely. "Do you realize, Auntie, he has taken us *miles* out of our way, and we will have to cross a river on a ferry to reach Bournemouth?"

Her aunt frowned in perplexity. "Has he, indeed? Why would he do such a cracker-brained thing?"

"Because finding Thomas is only a small part of his

reason for this trip. He came here to Fareham to look into the by-election. He suggested you and I continue to Bournemouth without him," she added, and looked for her aunt's reaction.

Delamar was not the only one with an ulterior motive for darting off to Bournemouth. Sharing Guy Delamar's company had been as much inducement as finding Lord Thomas, in the chaperone's decision. She hastily considered the matter and decided that laissez-faire was her best option. Who knew what might occur before morning? "We shan't go far tonight in any case. Did Delamar give a hint as to how long he meant to remain here?"

"Till his business is finished," Faith said tartly.

"Your trip with Guy was less than agreeable, if I am to judge by your sour face," Lady Lynne remarked.

"I did not want to join him and he didn't want me in his rig. I don't know why you ever suggested such a thing."

Lady Lynne plopped down on the bed and leveled a cool stare at her niece. "Then you are remarkably slow, my dear. The Season has less than two weeks to run. The only gentleman who offered for you has turned out to be a thief."

"Thomas is not a thief!"

"He's under a cloud at least. Your papa will never permit the wedding to take place now. By sheer good luck, a better replacement has dropped in your path and you haven't the wits to throw your bonnet at him. I have chaperoned some slow lasses in my life, but I must say, Faith, you take the prize. If all the chits were as dull as you, the bells of St. George's in Hanover Square would be silent from head to toe of the year."

Faith stiffened up and glared. "Are you actually suggesting that I should make up to that—that *scribbler*? I don't want to marry Mr. Delamar. I don't care for him in the least."

"Then it will be back to Mordain Hall for you, come June. Now that I have made Guy's acquaintance, I might attach him for Hope—if Lady Marie Struthers don't beat me to him, that is to say." She removed her bonnet and walked to the window to survey the skies and to give Faith time to come to her senses.

"Don't think you will talk Hope into having him," Faith sneered. "She will not be impressed by a Whig reformer—and neither will Papa." Yet she felt hypocritical casting a slur on Mr. Delamar's views.

"What has marriage to do with politics, you silly chit! Marriage is business, my dear. You will find your papa don't look too closely at a man's politics if the dibs are in tune."

"Then I pity Hope, having to live in a squalid room over that noisy paper."

This brought a pensive frown to Lady Lynne's face. "If he actually lives there, then he must have salted away a good deal of blunt. They say in town that he is making a fortune. I wonder if Struthers has already hinted he means to set him up in a house. . . ." This notion was dark enough to worry her.

While they were still discussing the matter, there was a knock at the door. Faith opened it to find the subject of their talk standing with his hat in his hand. "Are the accommodations satisfactory, ladies?" he asked.

"Fine, thank you," Faith replied.

Her aunt was more effusive. "Excellent. Come in, Guy, and let us discuss what is to be done next."

"I thought you might appreciate tea after the trip and have arranged for it to be served in a parlor below."

"That's mighty thoughtful of you." Lady Lynne beamed. "We shall be there in the twinkling of a bedpost."

He left, and Lady Lynne hastened to the mirror to adjust her coiffure. Over her shoulder she said, "Pretty good manners for a scribbler."

The ladies soon went downstairs and found Mr. Delamar waiting for them in the lobby. He was not alone, but Faith found it hard to believe the elegant gentleman with him could be his employee. The man had an air of breeding and distinction. He wore the buckskins and top boots of a county man, but he was done up in impeccable style. Customers in the lobby turned to look at the two tall, handsome young men speaking in somewhat excited voices and shaking hands as though long-lost friends.

Delamar saw the ladies from the corner of his eye and beckoned them forward. "Look who I found in the taproom, ladies. I expect you are acquainted with His Grace?" he asked. Their blank and startled faces told him he was wrong in this assumption. "The Duke of Graveston. Harry, this is Lady Lynne and her niece, Lady Faith Mordain."

The duke bowed, the ladies curtsied, and all three examined each other with the liveliest curiosity. Lady Lynne was not one to leave curiosity unsatisfied and plunged in to learn what freak of chance had made a duke and a commoner bosom bows, for that appeared to be the relationship between the men.

"The Duke of Graveston," she said, trying to place this prominent peer. "But of course, you are old Gouty Graveston's son. Your country seat is nearby, if I am not mistaken?"

"Not two miles away. You knew my late papa?" he asked with interest.

The acquaintance had not been close enough for her to know that the old duke was dead, but as he was, she was free to claim any degree of intimacy she wished. "I knew him very well. A delightful gentleman," she answered without blinking. "I was so sorry, to hear of his passing. And do you come from this part of the country, Guy?" She figured Guy's family must have worked for Graveston.

"No, I am from London," he answered unhelpfully.

"How did the two of you ever manage to meet and become friends? You don't spend much time in London, Your Grace."

"I am indebted to my youngest brother for the acquaintance," His Grace explained. "Guy was his colonel in the Peninsula." Faith heard the word *colonel* and her head jerked to look at Mr. Delamar. A colonel! He wasn't looking at her, but she felt he was aware of her shock all the same. The duke spoke on. "Young Beau caught a bullet in his leg, and Guy brought him home when the war was

63

over. We feel Beau owes his life to Guy. Beau is not the only one, either. But of course you ladies know your companion is the hero of Salamanca. I don't have to tell you about his attack—"

Guy interrupted swiftly. "This is not the place to discuss war. Won't you join us for tea, Harry?"

"I could do with a cup," he agreed, and the group made its way to the private parlor.

When they were seated, the duke tried to return to the topic of war, but Guy diverted him with a question. "What do you figure are our chances of dumping Shaft, Harry?"

"I've done what I can to bring our man to prominence," the duke said, and was easily diverted to this subject. "My people will vote for Makepiece, of course. I took him around to speak at any meeting that promised more than three votes, but Shaft is very strongly entrenched hereabouts after his father's three terms in office. He's had plenty of time to buy friends. A pity I hadn't a rotten borough to offer you, but then I know your views on that subject. Is it the election that brings you to Fareham?"

"That's one of the reasons," Guy answered.

Faith felt her heart shrink in her breast. The whole ugly story would come out now. Delamar would naturally make inquiries to learn if Thomas had been seen in the neighborhood. The story always came first with him. It made her realize just how unpleasant life would be as the bride of a man with a stain on his character—even an undeserved stain.

"Are you ladies that keen on politics that you are here for the same reason?" the duke asked. "Or am I being even more obtuse than usual?" he added, smiling from Faith to Guy. He was obviously seeking to discover if there was an understanding between them. Their eyes met; Guy saw the mute plea in hers.

"I am accompanying the ladies to Bournemouth to visit relatives," Guy said blandly. Lady Lynne breathed a sigh of relief, and Faith lowered her gaze. She felt a gush of gratitude to this enigmatic man who could always surprise her.

"If you're in no hurry, I'd be delighted to put you all up at the Hall," the duke offered. "Do come, Guy. The trout streams are begging to be fished. And Beau will have my head on a pike if I let you get away without bringing you home. A day seldom passes that he doesn't speak of you."

Lady Lynne smiled her acquiescence at this unexpected treat. A visit to a ducal mansion took precedence over even her five thousand pounds.

"Perhaps on the way back," Guy said. "We are in a bit of a hurry, and I must be in town tonight."

"I see what it is. The story! But you have a man here to cover that. I've met Fletcher. He seems a bright fellow— he can handle it."

"The ladies are expected in Bournemouth tomorrow" was Guy's next excuse.

"A day or two can't make any difference."

Guy smiled easily at the ladies. "We men are all alike, you are thinking. I daresay Lady Faith's aunt has killed the fatted calf and arranged flowers and a rout party. A few days can make quite a difference to a fatted calf and a bouquet of flowers."

"Then you must stop on your way back to London after you have delivered the ladies, Guy," the duke insisted.

"I'll stop to say hello, but I am a working man, you know."

"The *Harbinger*, of course. You're doing a bang-up job, by the by. I never miss an issue, but I wish I could get ahold of it earlier."

"Buy a subscription. I have it sent out on the mail coach."

"By Jove, I will!" he said, and reached in his pocket for money. "Clair enjoys your Mam'selle Ondit column, too. I have a tidbit for it if you're interested in country doings. I have asked her to marry me, and she, being of unsound mind, has accepted."

"Congratulations!" Guy said, and shook his hand. "My best wishes to you both. Be sure to tell Clair how happy I am."

"Clair who?" Lady Lynne asked.

"Lady Clair Claversham," the duke said, smiling fondly.

"That will be sorry reading in London—that one of the country's most eligible bachelors has been caught in the parson's mousetrap," Lady Lynne said.

"You must come for the wedding. It is to be held in a month," the duke said to Guy. They discussed this and other matters for half an hour, then the duke left, repeating his invitation to visit.

"What a fine fellow he is," Lady Lynne said with a sigh, "and what a pity these prime *partis* hide themselves in the country during the Season." Then she turned her sharp gaze to Delamar. "You're a sly rascal, sir, pretending to be no one when you are in the habit of hobnobbing with dukes and duchesses."

"I must differ, milady. I never called myself 'no one.' I am not famous enough for such humility. That opinion was your own, based, I must assume, on what you saw."

"What was one to think when what she saw was that miserable little cubbyhole under the eaves of your paper? Where do you really live, Guy?"

"I have a house in London," he said vaguely.

Faith cleared her throat nervously and said, "I did not realize you were a colonel, and a hero."

"I thought you would say an officer and a gentleman," he answered archly. "The mystery is easily explained, if you are interested. I didn't buy the commission. I won it on the field of battle—in the poor man's way."

"But you must have been an officer at least," Lady Lynne pointed out. "They do not promote privates or corporals to colonels for no reason."

"I was a lieutenant, then a captain and a major. The promotions were not given for no reason, but usually because my superior officer on the field was killed. It was a hard campaign."

An uncomfortable silence settled around them. Guy obviously did not want to talk about the war, and though Faith felt an urge to apologize, she didn't know how to do

66

it without emphasizing her own obtuseness. She could at least show some regard for his present comfort and chose to break the silence in that way. "Where will you spend the night?" She turned to her aunt and explained, "There was only one chamber free at the inn, and Mr. Delamar insisted we have it."

"I've arranged to bivouac with Fletcher."

Lady Lynne quietly observed the new mood of ingratiation in her niece and, like a good officer herself, planned her maneuver. "I must run up and have a rest. I'm rattled to death from travel. You finish your tea, Faith. Shall we meet in the morning, Guy, or must you remain in Fareham a little longer? Faith said something about our going on alone."

"I can leave by nine, if you want to delay your departure that late. Thomas's ship doesn't leave till evening." He looked a question at Faith. She felt the decision rested in her hands.

Officer Lynne felt the same and hastened to preempt it. "Nine! Good gracious, I doubt if I'll be out of my bed so early." She laughed and then whisked adroitly from the parlor. There, she had cornered the quarry, and if she was any judge of a man's eyes, he was no unwilling quarry, either. She may not weary her eyes with books, but she read faces with great discernment. Whether her niece had the wits to vanquish him was still a matter of grave doubt.

Faith stayed behind, but her first speech was "I must leave, too." This said, she did not arise but instead poured another cup of tea. "Before I go," she said uncertainly, "I want to apologize if I've said anything . . . unkind."

"You said what you thought. Truth takes precedence over kindness," he said, rather stiffly.

"But I thought the wrong things! It was very kind of you not to tell the duke about Thomas. I appreciate that, Mr. Delamar."

Her hope was to break down the wall of reserve that surrounded them, but her words seemed to have the opposite effect. The harder she tried to soften him, the stiffer he grew. His face was harsh and his voice like ice when, after a noticeable pause, he finally spoke. "You don't have to thank me. It isn't time to break the story yet. I have no proof that Thomas is guilty. I have suspicions, and a journalist can bankrupt himself in libel suits if he prints his suspicions as fact. When I have proved beyond a doubt that Lord Thomas is a thief, I'll print it and let the chips fall where they may."

She listened without anger and without surprise. "I know you will. The story always comes first."

"Especially this story," he said grimly.

She sensed the angry tension in him and knew it must have a more personal reason than the love of truth and justice. A man's eyes didn't glow like live coals over inanimate truth unless he was mad. "Why *this* story especially? Did you put money in the Afro-Gold Company yourself?"

"Certainly not. I'm not an idiot. I learned long ago that money doesn't fall from the sky. Good, honest, hard work goes into it, unless a man is a scoundrel," he added, with a thought of Lord Thomas. "I didn't invest, but I know a couple of fellows who did—young men who were officers under my command. The habit of responsibility dies hard. One of them lost a leg at Badajoz and is having trouble finding regular work. He put his life savings into the Afro-Gold Company—that's Eddie Proctor. He has a wife and two children. Buck Bellows is—well, he took a bullet in the head and his brain suffered from it. He isn't able to work. Buck isn't married. He has a mother and two sisters to support. At the moment, they're all living on his officer's half pay in three hired rooms. Your Thomas may be innocent. For your sake I hope he is, but someone is guilty. And by God, whoever he is, he'll pay."

The determination, the vehemence of his words sent a shiver up her spine. She had never seen such an implacable face, but in such a cause she admired his determination. "How awful for them, Mr. Delamar," she said softly. "Can nothing be done to help . . ." Then she stopped as she realized that this was the reason he was here, chasing Thomas. Thomas couldn't have taken money from

68

wounded veterans, no one but a monster would do such a thing. She drew a breath sadly and turned her gaze away from Guy.

When he spoke, his rough voice had turned suddenly gentle. "It may seem hard—unbearable at the moment. I know what it is to love in vain, Faith," he said softly. She felt the prick of curiosity. Who had he loved? What sort of woman had incited this man to passion? His hand moved across the table and gripped hers. He had never called her by her given name before. On his lips, it sounded warm and intimate. She looked at him in alarm and felt she was observing a stranger. The harshness was gone, leaving a tender glow in his savage eyes. "But if Lord Thomas is what I think he is, you're better off without him. Only think if you had married him and then learned he was not a man you could love and admire."

She looked at their clasped hands. Hers looked small and white and vulnerable in his strong fingers. "Thomas is not what you think, Mr. Delamar," she said simply.

He immediately withdrew his hand. The moment of intimacy was over, and he reverted to his ironic, mocking mood. "There is none so blind as she who will not see. As Shakespeare said, 'Men have died from time to time, and worms have eaten them, but not for love.' It applied to ladies as well. You'll get over him. Next year, Mam'selle Ondit will be writing about the nuptials of Lady Faith with some other gentleman if he cannot report her marriage to Lord Thomas this Season."

"Don't bet any money on it," she said brusquely.

"Why not? I'm a betting man. If you're as certain as you say, let's place a bet."

"I don't have any money—to spare, I mean. Besides, I've never bet on anything in my life."

He reached for her hand again, her left hand this time, and fingered her engagement ring. "Bet me this. If you're wrong, you'll be happy to be rid of it, and if you're right, you get it back."

"I told you, I don't wager."

"As far as you're concerned, it's not a real wager. A

69

wager involves taking a risk on an uncertain event. You *do* entertain some doubts then. . . ."

"No! I'll wager if you like. What do you bet on your part?"

"The monetary value of the ring—about a hundred guineas, I'd say at a guess."

"Done!" she said angrily.

"Clap hands on a bargain." He smiled and tried to remove the ring.

"I'll hold the wager. You can trust me," she said, closing her fingers over the ring.

"Yes, but that's not what . . ." She looked a question at him, and he came to a self-conscious stop. "You are still constant in your affection, then?"

"Papa always encouraged us to develop the special attribute of our names. Mine, as you know, is Faith."

"You'll need it," he cautioned, still in that mocking tone.

"Then Papa was right in advising me to develop it. I must go now. Good day."

She left the room, deeply dissatisfied with his parting words. Her original disgust of Mr. Delamar had gradually eased to acceptance. She had grudgingly come to respect his views when she read his paper and to admire his courage when she learned he was a war hero. She could understand his wanting to help his friends—even admire it. Why couldn't he understand she must be firm, too, in her protection of Thomas? She regretted having made the bet with him and wondered what he had been about to say before he changed his mind.

When she entered the room, her aunt was not lying down but rooting through her valise, selecting a change of gown. It was Faith who claimed fatigue and went to the bed. It was impossible not to think of Thomas. She had cringed lest Mr. Delamar announce that he was her fiancé and a thief. What if he was? What if she had given her love, and her freedom, to such a creature? She carefully considered what she actually knew of Lord Thomas Vane.

He was handsome, the handsomest man she had ever

70

seen. He was lively and fun. But did he have that some-what necessary item, character? She knew in her bones that Thomas, though a younger son with few prospects, would never have joined the army and gone to fight for his country. He liked high living too much. He liked pretty girls—she remembered, with a stab of anger, the red peignoir—and gambling, fast horses and parties. Those things cost a great deal of money. But would he steal to obtain them? She must have faith in him. Nothing was proven. A dull ache was in her heart. Nothing was proven, but the doubt was there where it had not been before, gnawing at the edges of her love.

Chapter Six

A cup of tea, even when taken with a charming young duke, was not enough nourishment to see that fine trencherman, Lady Lynne, through the night. She must go to the bother of rigging herself up in an evening outfit and the expense of hiring a parlor and ordering dinner herself, but even this wasn't enough to deter her.

"Why don't we have dinner sent up here instead?" Faith suggested.

"Dull! The inn is alive with patrons due to the election. We shall go below. Who knows, we might run into some acquaintance. Sir John had any number of relatives and friends in this area. Come along, child, scramble into your gown. There is no need to worry over your curls. Delamar will not see you tonight." Sliding a surreptitious glance at her niece, she noticed the self-conscious look that took possession of her face. "I wonder what he is up to," she added.

"Meeting with Mr. Fletcher, I expect, and preparing his article on the election here."

"Perhaps we'll bump into them downstairs," the dame said hopefully.

They went below and spoke to the proprietor. A private parlor was not immediately available, which suited Lady Lynne down to the heels since it gave her an excellent excuse to loiter about the lobby and peruse the gentlemen there. A carefully arranged accident with her shawl, catching it on the elbow of a handsome squire as she whisked past him, brought about her first new acquaintance.

The gentleman picked up the fallen shawl and handed it to her, but was soon made to realize he was expected to help with its placement over her shoulders. While he performed this office, she smiled and said, "I have never seen a small inn so busy. What can be going on here?"

Her niece was aware, after six weeks' residence with her aunt, that she was not expected to blurt out the answer, which was equally well known to them both.

"Why, we are in the middle of a by-election, ma'am," the man told her.

"Oh, politics!" Lady Lynne exclaimed, and quickly pondered whether to display a maidenly ignorance, which would permit the man to enlighten her, or a worldly knowledge, to put them on an equal footing. A provincial, she decided, would prefer his women ignorant. "Are they electing a new cabinet minister? I heard nothing of it in London."

A pair of bright country eyes danced gleefully at her stupidity. "Nothing so grand, madam. Only a simple M.P."

He appeared to be on the verge of continuing on his way, and she hastily threw in a remark to detain him. "That would be why my niece and I have to wait for a vacant parlor, then," she said. "I assure you we are not accustomed to standing around in inn lobbies, chatting to strangers. But at least we may overcome the latter impropriety. I am Lady Lynne and this is my niece, Lady Faith Mordain."

"Squire Brody, at your service, melady," he said, and bowed deeply.

"So kind of you," she crooned. "Do you have something to do with the election, Mr. Brody? I don't want to keep you from your duties."

"Nothing official, though I am a very interested constituent. You will see half the town collected here, waiting to hear the results."

Faith, hoping to hear something of use to Mr. Delamar,

intruded herself into the conversation. "Who do you think will win, Mr. Brody?"

"Oh, Young Shaft, for a certainty. It is only the confirmation we are waiting to hear, and then we shall begin celebrating in earnest. We expect to see Shaft come, smiling, through the door at any moment now."

Lady Lynne heard the name Shaft for the first time and it sounded familiar to her. "Not George Shaft?" she asked.

"No, old George's passing away is what brought on the by-election. It is his son Willie who took up the standard for him. Are you acquainted with the family, then?"

"Connected slightly on my late husband's side. My husband, Sir John Lynne, was an M.P. before he passed away."

"Then you will want to meet young Willie," Mr. Brody said.

A country member young enough to be her son was of little interest to Lady Lynne, so she did not press this issue. It was again Faith who thought it might be put to Delamar's advantage. "We should very much like to offer him our congratulations," she said.

The proprietor came forward and told them their parlor was now available. Lady Lynne invited Mr. Brody to take a glass of wine with them, but he was more interested in talking to his friends and declined. They were led to a small parlor a little out of the way. By leaving the door open, they had a view of new arrivals at least. A good meal was always enough to divert Lady Lynne, but Faith was preoccupied. The wind howled wildly past the windows, and the slash of rain against the panes was upsetting. Though she still had Thomas to worry about, it was Mr. Delamar who was at the top of her thoughts. She wondered what he was doing out on such a stormy night. But then he was accustomed to hardship—what would he care for a mere storm when he was used to being shot at? It must have been the war that gave him that hardened appearance she found so disagreeable. Yet he could be tender, too, at times. Was he tender with that other woman, the one he had loved in vain? She pictured a señorita with flashing black eyes. That would be the sort of woman to appeal to Mr. Delamar.

Their dinner was eaten and removed. While Lady Lynne sipped her wine and considered the advantage of apple tart versus gingerbread and gooseberry preserves for dessert, a commotion in the hall beyond alerted them to a new arrival at the inn. She leaned forward to see who had entered, then pushed back her chair. "It's Guy!" she exclaimed happily. "Soaked to the skin. He looks as though he's just been fished out of the sea. Someone's with him." She ran to the door and called him in.

He was, indeed, thoroughly drenched. His black hair was plastered against his head and water dripped from his shoulders. He stopped at the door and bowed. "Good evening, ladies. I'm happy to see you managed to get a parlor. I was afraid you might be consigned to your chamber for the entire evening."

"Come in, come in," Lady Lynne urged. "Join us, if you haven't eaten. You'll never get a parlor. We had to wait an age."

Behind him in the doorway lurked another soaking-wet man. "We're in no condition to join you," Guy said, mopping his brow with a handkerchief, but his eyes turned to Faith to read her mood.

"Mr. Delamar must change, Auntie. He'll catch his death of cold if he doesn't."

"It's only our outer coats that are soaked," he pointed out, and removed his to show a dry jacket, though the bottom of his trousers was a shade darker than the top and Faith was convinced his boots were soaked through.

"Why, you're dry as a desert," Lady Lynne declared. "Come and join us and tell us what you've been up to. There is plenty of room for you both."

"If you're sure we won't crowd you . . ." he said, again looking to Faith. She smiled a small welcome, and it was settled but for the gentlemen to run up to Fletcher's room to towel-dry their hair. Even Lady Lynne's eagerness for company allowed them that small vanity.

When they returned, they were wearing clean shirts and

cravats and a scent of some spicy cologne hovered around them. Guy introduced the ladies to his employee, Dick Fletcher. His skin was the same heathenish color as his companion's, though his blond hair and blue eyes proclaimed him an Englishman even before he spoke. His accent proclaimed him a gentleman.

"Dick and I were together in Spain," Guy said briefly. He never said more than the minimum on that subject. "Dick does some of my best pieces for the *Harbinger*, especially on politics."

"What have you learned about the election here?" Faith asked, aiming her question between the two men.

"We've learned plenty," Fletcher said, "but proving it is something else again. The election was certainly rigged—it began at the polling booth, before the returns were taken for counting. The usual preelection tricks were carried out as well, of course. Bribery, treating, perhaps a little coercion here and there."

"Treating?" Lady Lynne asked. "I never heard Sir John speak of that. Is it something new?"

"As old as Adam," Mr. Fletcher replied. "The non-Tory voters are wined and dined to such excess before the election that they aren't in shape to stumble to the polls. But even with that help, the Tories weren't sure of taking it. Guy and I hung around outside the returning officers' window, trying to see what went on. Graveston kicked up such a fuss that the Whig was allowed a representative in on the counting."

"I'm by no means sure the scrutineers weren't stuffing a few votes into their pockets or up their sleeves," Guy added. "It was hard to see through the window with the rain pouring down. We're interested to see the final count. Dick's taken his own unofficial poll and he figures it should be a close call. If the Tories come in with some inordinate majority, we'll know they juggled the count."

"And we won't be able to print it because we have no proof," Dick added, shaking his head in frustration.

Faith listened with the keenest interest, and when a silence fell, she said, "My aunt is slightly acquainted with

76

the Shaft family. Sir John was a Tory M.P., as you know, Guy.'' The name slid out unawares, but Mr. Delamar noticed and smiled. She thought his pleasure was in her news and continued eagerly. ''If she could talk to him privately—well, I don't suppose he'd crop out into a confession, but he might speak fairly freely with another Tory.''

''But would a Tory lady relay her findings to the *Harbinger*?'' he asked, leveling a conning smile at the chaperone, who cared no more for politics than she cared for higher mathematics.

Her inane laughter cheered the gentlemen immensely. ''Lud, it's the least I can do after all your help the past few days.'' And, with luck, his continued help. The bill for dinner had not been presented yet.

A waiter appeared and the men ordered their dinner. While Guy and Fletcher attacked beefsteaks, the ladies enjoyed their apple tart and coffee, and they all laid plans to con Mr. Willie Shaft into indiscretion.

''It's a pity old George upped and died. Him I could have handled,'' Lady Lynne said. ''It is his son we're dealing with now, and I've never even met the man, though I can reasonably present myself to him as a friend of his papa. What is Willie like?''

It was Dick Fletcher who had been busy learning about the candidate. ''A bumptious, ignorant farmer who'll go up to London and vote as he's told so long as the local patronage is given to him.''

''Yes, but what is he *like*?'' Lady Lynne repeated. ''Is he married? Is he a toper, a womanizer? Is he handsome?'' she added, from habit.

Guy grinned. ''Single, not overly abstemious or misogynistic, not a bad-looking gent. About twenty-six or seven,'' he added. Such was his opinion of Lady Lynne that he looked to see if she was ready to tackle him.

''Then it will be for Faith to take him on,'' the dame said.

''Me?'' Faith objected. Her protest was hardly louder than Mr. Delamar's, though it was voiced in a higher tone.

''It won't be necessary to involve Lady Faith in anything

of the sort," he said firmly. "A postelection party is no place for a lady like Faith."

She noticed the angry flush on his cheeks and the hot glance he shot at her. He thought she'd make a botch of it—that's what was bothering him. He didn't think she was capable of enchanting a man just because *he* didn't like her. She knew she wasn't outgoing, but with a provincial like Willie Shaft, she would be able to flirt.

"There's hardly a sober soul in the inn already and the results aren't even in yet," Mr. Fletcher added.

"That's true," Guy agreed. "In fact, I strongly recommend you ladies go to your rooms. I'll accompany you up."

"Good gracious," Lady Lynne said with a laugh, "the provincials of Fareham can hardly be so wicked that you must interrupt your dinner to take us up now." She regarded the two young bucks and had no desire whatsoever to leave the table. "In fact, I mean to have another sliver of that apple tart."

She ladled a five-inch sliver onto her plate and proceeded to gobble it up, before offering at least to make Guy and Mr. Fletcher known to Willie Shaft as soon as she had met him herself.

"If we happen to meet him on the way to your room," Guy agreed. "But for God's sake, don't tell him who we are."

"I'm Dick Fletcher, a shipping magnate in a very small way," Fletcher informed her.

"I'm a colleague, Mr. Charles by name."

A judicious dawdling till the candidate was heard entering the inn made the introduction possible. By this time, the taproom had flowed over into the lobby and the crowd—all male except for Faith and her chaperone and a few members of the muslin company—was becoming rowdy but not so out of hand that they failed to make a path for the ladies.

In the distance, Faith could see that there were women in the throng and said to Guy, "We aren't the only ladies here after all."

"Yes, you are," he answered firmly.

"If those persons in skirts are not ladies, pray what are they?" she asked.

He looked down and smiled quizzically. "How old are you, Lady Faith?"

"I'm eighteen. Why?"

"Eighteen? Then the persons in skirts are actresses," he said, and laughed when the truth dawned on her.

Guy pointed out Mr. Shaft, a tall, gangly country fellow with brown hair and a sallow complexion.

Lady Lynne strode boldy up to him. "Mr. Shaft, allow me to introduce myself and to congratulate you on your coming victory." She smiled brightly. "My husband and I were close friends of your dear late papa. Sir John knew George forever—from the egg. I am the widow of Sir John Lynne." She went on to qualify herself as a staunch Tory lady. The obvious conclusion was that her companions were also true blue. There was not such a surfeit of "ladies" in Fareham that Mr. Shaft resented her support. His chest swelled in pleasure to be so flattered in front of his friends.

Guy and Fletcher edged up beside her and were presented as friends. "You've heard of the Fletcher-Charles shipping line, of course," she added. "Mr. Charles is thinking of switching some of his cargo to your port here at Fareham. Perhaps you can do a little something to help him, eh, Mr. Shaft?" she added.

Shaft's shifty eyes slid to examine the pair for possible mutual benefit and shook their hands. He next spotted Lady Faith, who stood smiling demurely at him. "You haven't made me acquainted with this young lass," he said to Lady Lynne.

"My niece, Lady Faith Mordain," she said.

Shaft stepped forward and made a stiff bow. Faith curtsied and cast a coquettish glance at him. "It's such a thrill to meet a real M.P., Mr. Shaft," she cooed.

"I'm not confirmed yet," he pointed out, but the goatish gleam in his eyes told her he didn't object to her assuming him victorious.

"I'm sure you will be. The voters of Fareham couldn't vote for anyone else when they have *you* to lead them."

His chest swelled perceptibly, and he placed her hand on his arm to cut her off from the others. "That's very kind of you to say so, my dear. Do you come to this part of the country often?"

"I haven't . . . till now. I never had any reason to."

"Perhaps we can find a reason, then," he said.

The crowd was closing in on them, which gave him an excuse to put an arm around her waist and help her through. She felt his fingers tighten noticeably and quelled the instinct to call him to order. Instead she smiled sweetly.

"How long are you staying, Lady Faith? Perhaps we could get together later for a good cose."

"And you can tell me all about how you got elected," she agreed.

He gave a cynical laugh. "Aye, there's a story there, right enough."

"I bet you did something wickedly clever!" she approved. "Papa says one Tory know more tricks than all the Whigs combined."

"There's something in that."

She looked a question at him, but before more could be said, Mr. Delamar was there, physically removing Shaft's hand from her arm and saying "Your aunt is waiting for you" in a rather imperative voice.

"Good night, Mr. Shaft. Perhaps we can talk again soon," Faith said.

"That we will, milady." He performed a rustic bow and was soon engulfed by his well-wishers.

Faith turned a quizzing eye on Delamar. "That was an untimely intrusion, sir. I had him in the palm of my hand."

She received no compliment, only an angry glower. "It wasn't the palm of *your* hand that concerned me. It was his, the mushroom. Why did you do it?"

Heady with her small success, she shrugged her shoulders and said airily, "Perhaps to show you that I could bring a man around my finger as well as the next lady if I wanted to."

He blinked in surprise. "To show *me* a lesson, in fact?"

"It's time someone did, Mr. Delamar," she bantered.

A reluctant smile entered his eyes. "That particular one was redundant. I'm already aware of your powers."

"I saw the look on your face when Auntie suggested it. You didn't think I could do it."

"I didn't think you *should* do it—there's a difference. You ladies must remove yourselves from this melee before it turns rough. Fletcher and I are known now and can return later."

With the utmost reluctance, Lady Lynne allowed herself and Faith to be shepherded through the throng and taken to their room. She attached herself to Guy, which left Faith to follow with Mr. Fletcher.

"This is very kind of you," Fletcher said. "From the way Guy's been talking, I didn't expect you ladies to take any active part in this job."

"My family are Tories," she admitted, "but since reading the *Harbinger* . . . It is very shocking, that business of whole families having to go out to work in the north of England. And the corn laws, too! I want to learn more about politics."

"Wanting is the beginning of getting, Guy says. Only look how he has proven the axiom. He has worked his way up from nothing to become one of the most influential men in England. Politicians come begging for his help. I shouldn't be too surprised to see him prime minister one day. He'd make a fine one, don't you think?"

She gave the question serious consideration before answering. His broad back proceeded up the stairs in front of her. "Yes, I think he would," she admitted slowly.

Fletcher smiled down at her. "He'll be happy to hear you think so, Lady Faith. He's taken the unaccountable notion that you despise him because he is a self-made man."

"Oh, no! That's not true! I admire him—I mean, a man who works his way up. I am not so priggish, Mr. Fletcher!"

"No doubt he misunderstood something you said. Most

people speak loosely. In the office Guy has a motto. He's a great gun for axioms and mottoes. 'We must write not only so that our meaning can be understood, but so clearly that it cannot possibly be *mis*understood.' Of course, no one is that precise in everyday speech,'' he added.

''You have a high opinion of your employer, I think?''

''Guy's the best friend a man ever had. I'd trust him with my life. Well, I have, more than once in Spain, and as you can see, I am still alive and kicking. The oddest thing is that he hates war, yet he was so good at it. I suppose he just hated more the possibility of being under Boney's heel. And him half a Frenchie. Odd, is it not, the tricks life plays on us?''

''Half French?'' she asked, startled.

''Yes, on his papa's side. His father was Jean de Lamare. They changed their name when they escaped to England during the Revolution. Guy is short for Guillaume, of course.''

''But it was only the aristocrats who fled from Robespierre!'' she exclaimed.

''No, he's not of noble blood. His father was originally against the aristocracy—a member of the moderate Gironde party, but when Robespierre went to such lengths, his father spoke out against him and had to flee for his life. Guy hasn't a good word to say for the aristocracy. He feels the Revolution in France was their fault, but, of course, the whole thing got out of hand in the end. No sane person ever intended for it to go so far.''

''Guy actually grew up in France then,'' she said.

''He says he was old enough to remember the horror of it, too young to do anything about it. That is his definition of frustration: to recognize a wrong and be powerless to correct it. His greatest fear is that the insensitivity of the aristocracy here in England could lead to a similar sort of thing, but I think now that he's met a few of our English aristos, he feels differently. He has no love for Prinney, but then who has?''

When they reached the chamber, Lady Lynne had already entered. Guy held the door for Faith. She turned and looked at him, seeing him clothed for the first time in the new facts she had just learned. The Gallic strain was so obvious she wondered that she hadn't guessed it. The British sangfroid was noticeably absent in him. His eyes glowed with a Latin passion. It lend an added allure, that touch of foreign glamour.

"Thank you," she said softly. A tinge of pleasant curiosity was in her expression. "And good evening. Or should I say *au revoir*?" she added.

"*Au revoir*, by all means. At least I trust we shall be meeting again—very soon. Does your suddenly wandering into French mean Dick has been telling tales on me?"

"Only a very short tale. I wish the walk had been longer," she answered. "How does it come you never told us you were French?" A smile curved his lips. "No—don't say it! We never asked."

"I try to avoid the obvious. I was going to say my name ought to have told you."

"Oh, yes, from de Lamare, of course."

"No from *on dit*. I refer to my feminine alter ego. You look very lovely tonight in that blue gown, Faith. But just between us, I think I preferred you in the pale yellow you wore the night we waltzed. Was it only last night?"

Dick had strolled a discreet few yards down the hall, but Lady Lynne turned to see what was keeping Faith and the moment was over. The chaperone was disgusted with herself when she saw the rosy flush on her niece's cheeks and the soft gleam of pleasure in her eyes.

"Nine tomorrow, then?" Guy said, including them both in the question.

"Yes. Good evening."

Faith closed the door and Lady Lynne turned a sapient eye on her charge. "You're looking very pleased with yourself, miss. Have you been taking my advice and casting your net in Guy's direction?"

"Certainly not. Mr. Delamar doesn't want to marry me."

"I see" was all the dame said, but the answer was as welcome as manna in the wilderness. She saw clearly that

"I don't want to marry Mr. Delamar" had become "Mr. Delamar doesn't want to marry me." She had only to remove the negative, and the thing was done.

It firmed her decision to write a retraction of the engagement for the London papers. It ought to have been done sooner, before they left town. She did it that very night and had it posted to London. A broken engagement was an excellent excuse for their absence from the social scene during these few days if anyone began asking questions. She knew she was doing the proper thing, but lest her act cause a recrudescence of Faith's love for Thomas, she delayed telling her niece about it.

Chapter Seven

When the ladies opened their door in the morning to go downstairs, they saw that a door across the hall, three or four rooms down, was open as well.

"Good timing!" Lady Lynne smiled. "That is Guy's room—the one he is sharing with Fletcher. He pointed it out last night when we came up." She lingered for a moment till he came out, and Faith waited with her, her heart beating unsteadily.

It would be hard to say which was the more surprised when a young female, garmented in gaudy apparel that revealed her calling, issued from the door across the hall. She had tousled black hair and a raucous, caterwauling voice.

"A whole sovereign! Why, thank you ever so," the black-haired girl exclaimed, and laughed a rowdy laugh.

Faith stared and her aunt rushed in to whitewash the interlude. "Fletcher's doings," she scoffed angrily.

"They were both sharing that room!" Faith said. Innocent though she was, she had heard of lechery and was aware of what the woman represented.

From behind the door, a man answered. The door not only concealed his identity but muffled his voice as well, though his words were distinguishable. "Sure it's enough? You had a hard night."

"I've had worse. Look me up any time you're in the neighborhood," she said saucily, and turned to leave.

Lady Lynne pushed Faith back into the room and closed

their door. As soon as the female had passed, however, she opened it again—to see Mr. Fletcher just coming up the stairs, giving the lie to Lady Lynne's story.

Unaware of the contretemps, he stopped to say good morning. "Shaft won. A big majority—it's no surprise. I've arranged a parlor for breakfast any time you ladies are ready. I'll just give Guy's door a knock. He had a little business to attend to before leaving."

Faith gave him a haughty stare and said, "I believe you'll find Mr. Delamar is finished with his *business* now." She turned a brusque shoulder on the poor innocent man and strode down to the parlor. Had she been less upset, she would have remained in her room, but before this excellent snub occurred to her, she was already seated in the parlor and the gentlemen had entered.

When Fletcher told Guy that Lady Faith had turned into a block of ice overnight, he suspected she had seen the female but naturally hoped otherwise. He entered the parlor wearing a wary smile and expressing the hope that they had slept well. His own hagged condition—bleary eyes, pale cheeks—was put down to his visitor and the smile to the same reason. It was a very satisfied smile.

"Very well, thank you," Faith said, but her eyes skewered him to the spot. "I trust you also enjoyed your night."

"*Enjoy* is hardly the right word," he objected. "We had some success."

"So had Mr. Shaft, I hear," she replied, and picked up the menu. "Just coffee for me. Something has turned my stomach. I couldn't eat a bite."

"Perhaps it's just as well," he replied, assuming an indifference to match hers. "You weren't looking forward to the ferry crossing, as I recall. I don't have a weak stomach myself. I'll have gammon and eggs. How about you, Dick?"

"I don't have to cross water. I'll have beefsteak and a rider. That's an egg atop," he explained to the waiter.

Foreseeing a difficult day, Lady Lynne ordered the same. She trusted that if Delamar was a libertine (and what man was not, at heart?), he was at least clever enough to have invented a story to satisfy Faith by now.

To give him an opening for his tale, she asked, "So you had no luck with Shaft last night?"

"We did and we didn't," he said, but his smile didn't look like failure. "We got him foxed enough to admit to a couple of dyed-in-the-wool Tories like Charles and Fletcher that he had rigged the election by the old tried-and-true stunts. Proving it is more difficult. If I understand his ravings aright, his returning officers went into the counting room with their pockets stuffed with ballots marked in his favor. They substituted them for real ballots, snaffling the others into their pockets when they had a chance, but that's only verbal admission and by a man who wasn't quite sober. We have no tangible evidence."

"So what is the outcome to be?" Lady Lynne demanded.

"Why, the outcome is that he will have to be unseated on some other charge."

"Such as?" Lady Lynne asked eagerly.

"Such as . . . this," he said, and tossed a letter onto the table.

She lifted it up and read it hastily. "The fool! Why would he put it in writing?" she demanded.

Faith was goaded into interest and took the letter written and signed in Mr. Shaft's own hand, from her aunt to read of an arrangement that for the vote of a Mr. Silas Barnes, he would promise Barnes the position of city clerk. "Patronage—is that illegal?" she asked, careful to direct her question to Mr. Fletcher.

"When it occurs in the opposition party, it is called bribery, which is indeed illegal," he assured her.

"How did you get the letter?"

"Shaft had it in his jacket pocket. He must have realized how dangerous it was and asked Barnes to give it back. He meant to destroy it, of course, but . . . well, he was in his cups last night and he didn't do it. This is not the only vote he bought, but one is enough to prove the point."

"What did you do, pick his pocket?" she asked. Her tone was far from approving.

"No, a . . . friend did it for us. A female, actually," Guy admitted.

"The one we saw at your door this morning?" Lady Lynne demanded. She was still on speaking terms with Guy and posed her question to him.

The scowl he turned on her might have intimidated a more sensitive soul, but it didn't faze Lady Lynne in the least. "You saw Millie, did you?" he asked. He risked a glance at Faith and had a good view of her averted jaw, set like Portland cement. "She stopped in for a minute this morning after—that is, before leaving the inn. Well, Willie is a bachelor, you know. It stands to reason that he'd want to celebrate his victory. And once he'd settled on Millie, we had a quiet word with her."

The cement jaw turned toward him. It unstuck long enough for Faith to say, in frigid accents, "I think it was a despicable thing to do."

"Are you referring to Willie Shaft or to me?" he asked bluntly.

"Both. Mr. Shaft has at least the excuse of being disguised."

"I consider public drunkenness an added offense myself. If I remember rightly, your attitude to a bachelor's entertaining a woman in his room was more lenient in London," he reminded her. "I did what I had to do. It is a case of the end justifying the means."

"What justifies the end? Who are you to play God with a man's career?"

"I am playing Justice, not God. We get the politicians we deserve. I don't deserve Shaft. If God wants to strike me dead and prevent my turning this letter over to the lord lieutenant, the Duke of Graveston, for handling, I shan't have a word to say against it."

"You *do* draw the line at overruling God, do you? I am surprised," she snipped.

"What will happen to Shaft?" Lady Lynne asked.

"He'll be disqualified from serving his term—perhaps

arrested and convicted of bribery, depending on how much influence he has. A new election will be held, and with the stink the *Harbinger* means to raise over the affair, the rerun will be handled with a deal more discretion."

"Couldn't you just threaten Shaft that if he doesn't resign . . . I am thinking of the man's reputation, his private life," Lady Lynne said.

"We are discussing his *public* life," Guy answered grimly. "When a man puts himself up for public office, he must set an example. He ought to be like Caesar's wife, above reproach. Politics needs the best men, not the scum."

Faith listened and felt a shiver dart up her spine. The man was implacable. He would have his story, and never mind who suffered. The easier way was not his way, not when there was a good story in it. "That should make lively reading," she said tartly.

"It will," he promised. "I see you ladies are displeased with me. It's the Shafts of the country who have brought us to the plight we're in."

"Our plight does not seem all that wretched to me," Faith said.

"You are one of the ten thousand, Lady Faith. In a country of ten million, ten thousand enjoy your privileges. That's one in a thousand, one tenth of one percent. For every Lady Faith, there are a thousand unfortunate Millies, is another way to look at it."

"How convenient for you bachelors!"

"The man's a criminal. I don't have to justify what I'm doing," he said angrily.

And Thomas, as far as Delamar was concerned, was just another criminal. He'd be equally intransigent with Thomas—even more so, given his hatred of aristocrats. Her feminine compassion was stirred on Mr. Shaft's behalf. Her own part in unmasking him was a further burr. Why had she done it? It was Delamar's air of rectitude that had impressed her, but how much of that air was real, honest rectitude and how much an excuse to persecute his enemies, to pillory them in print? And on her own side, she had to admit that she had helped him as much to gain his good opinion as to curb political chicanery.

Over breakfast, there was more discussion of the night's doings, but Faith hardly listened and said nothing. She remembered the angry lurch of her heart when she saw that woman issuing from Guy's room. It was worse than seeing the red peignoir in Thomas's flat. Were all men so horrid? How long had she been there? Long enough to do more than hand him an envelope, she figured. He wouldn't have sent Fletcher downstairs if that had been all their business together.

As they were in a hurry, there was no dawdling over breakfast. The ladies went upstairs to prepare their valises, while Guy gave some last-minute instructions to Fletcher before the latter returned to London. Lady Lynne, worried that she had been precipitate in mailing the cancellation of the engagement, immediately lit into her charge for her morose behavior at breakfast.

"That's a poor way to nab a fellow, miss! You'd think he'd stolen money, like Thomas, to judge by your Friday face."

"I expect he did worse than that, Auntie. Why did he send Fletcher away when that trollop was in his room?"

"The man is a bachelor, for goodness' sake. Men have appetites that you know nothing about. Don't they teach you chits anything in your seminary? All that sort of thing will stop once he's shackled—or it will if his wife has her wits about her."

"Then you *do* think he was . . ."

"It wouldn't surprise me. What's the harm in it? It's not as though that Millie person were an innocent girl. Entertaining gentlemen is her business. He paid her. What more do you want of him?"

"Less hypocrisy," Faith said. Her jaw again assumed its frozen, mulish angle. "He shouldn't preach so much piety if he's no better than the others. I thought he was something special—a war hero, a self-made man, a *good* man." Thomas at least had never assumed any air of rectitude. She knew him for a gazetted flirt.

"Pooh!" was her aunt's answer to what she considered pious fustian. "He is an excellent *parti*. There isn't a man alive who don't chase after skirts when he's away from home, Faith, and the sooner you learn it, the better. Why, if that is all that concerns you, you obviously don't know much about Thomas Vane."

"What about him?" she demanded swiftly.

"Lud, he's the worst womanizer in London. With his looks, he had his pick of them all, and he didn't turn down many, I can tell you."

"But you said he was unexceptionable!"

"He is—*was* unexceptionable for you. Do you think it's *easy* to find a husband for a country chit with no dowry to speak of and no extraordinary beauty? Your papa, the gudgeon, insisted on a title into the bargain. I'll tell you something I had hoped to keep from you, for otherwise you'll return to Mordain Hall a spinster. Thomas was not all that hot to have you, my girl. His papa insisted he marry or he'd not pay his debts. It was debtors' prison or you—those were Thomas's choices. It comes to seem he preferred a life of crime to marrying you, so you need not mount your high horses because Guy Delamar had a lightskirt in his room. There's a time to be wide awake and a time to close one eye. For you, this is a time to close one eye and not look too sharp out of the other."

Faith stared at her aunt with a disbelieving look. "But you said Thomas was unexceptionable! He told you he would be desolate if I refused him!"

"Aye, so he would. A mighty unpleasant hole, debtors' prison."

"He said he loved me," she added on a whisper.

"Hah! I wish I had a shilling for every silly chit he said that to."

"Then why are we here? Why are we following Thomas?"

"Because he has my five thousand guineas, that's why. And because I hoped you might nab Delamar, if we could get him alone, away from more desirable ladies," Lady

91

Lynne said baldly. Of course she did not mention her first hope of attaching him herself.

Faith turned away and began to shove clothing into her valise. Tears pricked at the back of her eyes, but by holding her breath and counting, she restrained them. Thomas didn't love her. He had never loved her. She was a last resort—no more. His handsome, dashing face, those eyes that had looked deep into hers and told her she was "a darling," had lied. She had been made a dupe by him and her aunt, and had made a fool of herself by praising him to Delamar. She wished she could crawl into the valise and have someone close and lock her inside, to avoid meeting Guy again. Not that he was any better!

Her face was long when they went downstairs to meet the gentlemen. Guy took Lady Lynne's valise from the page boy, and Mr. Fletcher took Faith's and led her to the carriage.

"Graveston has just picked up the letter and has gone after Shaft," Fletcher told her. "I daresay you find Guy's attitude a little intransigent. He's a soldier at heart, you know. They play for keeps. If you give your enemy a second chance, you end up very dead. He must have showed you the spent bullet he uses for a watch fob. It landed in his cheekbone on the occasion when he showed mercy to a wounded soldier in Spain. He kept it as a reminder. Shaft is a born scoundrel like his father before him. Bribery, corruption—every manner of crooked dealing. Guy wouldn't have sent me down to cover just any by-election. He's had his muzzle aimed on Shaft for a long time, ever since Graveston discovered the mishandling of affairs here. It would be asking too much to give Shaft another chance."

"I assure you I am not asking anything of Mr. Delamar," she said primly.

"He hoped you would not ask *that* favor, in any case. As to asking anything other than that . . . well, I shouldn't hesitate. He's generous. If you have much to do with him, you'll find he asks a good deal of you. He doesn't mind asking the impossible of people—the strangest thing is that they seldom refuse."

They reached the carriage, shook hands, and made their farewells. "I'm back to London to oversee getting out the rag. Perhaps I'll see you there later, Lady Faith? Are you making a long visit at Bournemouth?"

She gave him a startled look, surprised that Guy had not told his close friend about Thomas. "No, not long. We'll be back within a few days. Yes, I hope we meet again."

He stored her valise and helped her into the waiting carriage.

Chapter Eight

Guy's carriage was already pulling out of the yard, and before long they drew up to the dock where the barge was waiting. It was not large enough to take the two carriages and teams in one crossing.

Guy came to them to explain the procedure. "I'll go across first with my rig, then come back to accompany you. It helps to have an extra man with the horses in case they're poor sailors. Bournemouth is only another twenty-five miles after that. We'll be there for lunch."

Lady Lynne said all that was polite, while Faith studiously regarded the *Times*, whose words were a blur in front of her eyes. She continued to hide behind the paper after Guy left, while her aunt went for a stroll along the dock. Faith wanted to go home. Not to London, but home to Mordain Hall to hide herself. Her Season was over, and she had failed. Next year Hope would be sent forth but not without an enlightening discussion with her failed sister. Someone ought to warn debutantes about the jungle that awaited them in London. She had gone to town an innocent girl full of hopes. It had seemed, for a brief, halcyon month, that all her dreams were to come true. She had met her Prince Charming, had her offer of marriage, but now it had soured. She had only the disgrace of having accepted an offer from a rogue and the humiliation of facing society and her family. She hadn't even been able to hang on to her rogue.

She wished she could at least conceal from the world the

extent of Thomas's treachery. If she could find him and make him return the money . . . When had she accepted that he had indeed stolen it? No matter, she accepted it now. If Delamar caught him, there would be no hope of keeping the thing quiet. If Thomas would only return the money and invent some story to cover his strange flight, then his family might be saved the shame of having harvested a criminal and she the degradation of having loved one.

This hope took a strong hold of her. Outwitting Mr. Delamar added a further incentive: It would give her great pleasure to best him. But how could she set about doing it? She must try to find Thomas before Delamar did.

As the weather was still blustery and cold, her aunt soon returned to the carriage, and Faith tried to enlist her aid. "It will be an awful scandal if Thomas's thievery hits the papers. Delamar will blazon it in headlines for the whole world to read. His father and mother will be killed with shame. I wonder where he is."

Her aunt wore a pensive face. Unmentioned by Faith, but of some importance to the aunt, was the fact that she had sponsored this match. It was she who would bear the brunt of blame and whose judgment would be in question. Lady Lynne had some misgivings herself about how Guy would handle the story in his paper. But her greatest fear was for the harm it would do to her niece's chances. Now that Faith had managed to lose Guy's interest, yet another replacement must be found. "Holed up in some inn, I expect. They will be the first places Guy looks. Has Thomas any friends in the neighborhood?"

"No."

"Hmm." A crafty light beamed in Lady Lynne's eyes. Thomas was certainly at an inn, and Delamar would just as certainly find him unless she devised a scheme. Faith was of no use as a liar. Never having been a wife, she had not perfected the conjugal art of misleading a gentleman. It would be for herself to lead Guy a merry chase, while she found Thomas and got her money back. Of course she would try to talk him into returning the lot, but, failing that, she would at least have her share. Let the others fend for themselves. That self-seeking bounder would leap at the chance of getting away with most of his ill-gotten gains, and she doubted that Guy would bother to publish half a story if he had to omit the best part: that he had captured the thief.

While they were waiting for the barge to return, another carriage pulled up behind them at the wharf. It was a hired carriage, not at all elegant, and was full of noisy, clamoring women.

The man who sold tickets cast a jaundiced eye on the inferior carriage and strolled up to speak to Lady Lynne. "That's the crew from across the water who were shipped in yesterday to entertain the gentlemen come to town for the election. Lightskirts, the lot of them," he scoffed.

The ladies, vastly interested in this matter, stared at the carriage. The door opened, and two of the females descended to stroll up and down the beach. They recognized the black-haired wench as Millie, Guy's cohort in catching Willie Shaft. Millie was the prettier of the two, and certainly the noisier. She gamboled about like a lamb, careless of the wind that carried her skirts into the air. Yet despite her awful voice and her common behavior, Faith had to acknowledge that the girl was uncommonly pretty.

When the barge returned and Delamar hopped ashore, Millie dashed up to him. They stood together chatting for a few minutes, longer than was necessary just to say good day. Guy leaned toward her, talking eagerly, and Millie nodded her head in agreement with whatever he had to say. When he pulled something from his pocket and handed it to her, the ladies exchanged a significant look.

"I assume Guy was pleased with Millie's performance," Faith said grimly.

"It looks like it," her aunt agreed, "since he's buying a ticket for a repeat performance."

After his transaction was finished, he added further fuel to their anger by not approaching them but only helping the groom get their carriage and team aboard. His own team were experienced seamen, and had made no fuss about boarding an unsteady barge. Lady Lynne's horses were landlubbers and resisted with all their force. It took a long time to coax them onto the barge, and once they were aboard, they continued to be restive. All Guy's talent and all his time were required to keep them quiet.

The ladies were equally nervous. The barge seemed very small and the water exceedingly rough. The craft pitched and dipped till they were quite sure they were all going to end up in the cold sea. The wind carried balls of foam, which flew against their gowns and faces and destroyed their coiffures.

"Why don't you get into the carriage? You'll be more comfortable," Guy suggested.

"If we are going to drown, I prefer not to do it locked up in a carriage," Faith said grimly.

"The fresh air is all that is keeping that beefsteak where it belongs" was Lady Lynne's reply. A glance at her yellowing face told Delamar this was true. Knowing that ladies disliked casting up their accounts in front of a gentleman, he returned to the horses and left them alone.

As soon as the second crossing was accomplished, the ladies retired to their carriage and the trip continued. They were drawing close to their destination now. Thomas might be seen at any moment, and from both carriages eager eyes scanned the road for him. As they proceeded westward, they entered New Forest, the royal hunting ground set apart by William the Conqueror to hunt the tall deer. Had their trip been less harrowing, they would have enjoyed the view of ancient oaks, yews, and holly bushes that distinguished the forest. The scenery was varied by heath and even farmland, for the forest was not a real forest. But Lady Lynne was by no means recovered from the crossing. She felt chilled to the marrow by her damp clothes and sat with eyes closed, moaning occasionally.

When they drew near to Bournemouth, the rising ground, rich in pines, gave them a view of the city below nestled at the mouth of the little Bourne River at Poole Bay. The cliff line was interrupted by chines that split the rock open as it fell straight to the sea below. Bournemouth was coming into popularity as a watering place for invalids, who appreciated its garden setting and scenic beauty.

At their descent into the city, nerves drew taut. Already hotels were springing up along Holdenhurst Road. Where Holdenhurst Road becomes Bath Road, Delamar had his carriage stopped and came back to speak to the ladies. The Lansdowne Hotel was on their right, another on their left.

"If I read Lord Thomas aright," he said, "he'll be staying at one of the better establishments. Perhaps the Royal Bath—it's the only hotel on the East Cliff that has a view of the sea at any rate. I suggest you ladies go there to recover," he said as he noticed that Lady Lynne was still distressed.

Faith was loath to speak to him, but she was on thorns to learn his plans. "What are you going to do?" she asked.

"I'm going to check in and have lunch."

Lady Lynne got her eyes open long enough to give approval to this destination, and the carriages resumed motion. She noticed the Pleasure Gardens on her right and thought a walk there in the afternoon might resuscitate her. The hotel was not yet as full as it would be after the King's Garden Party on the fourth of June, which marked the official close of the Season. There were plenty of rooms, and when the ladies were taken upstairs, they were astonished to find that Mr. Delamar had hired them two adjoining rooms. From their windows, they looked out over the East Cliff Promenade to the sea. This was not where the boats would dock; it was the bathing place.

While Faith stood gazing at the vast expanse of water, all gray and shiny like crumpled steel, she heard a knock on her aunt's door. The voice that wafted through to her belonged to Mr. Delamar, which caused her spine to stiffen and her feet to remain frozen to the floor. She was sure she'd be called, and when this didn't happen, she was so incensed she refused to acknowledge knowing that he was there.

"Do you feel up to tackling lunch?" Guy asked the dame.

"Perhaps toast and tea, sent up here. I'm for a lie-down."

"What about Faith?" he asked hopefully. She noticed the reluctant interest, and her hopes in that direction revived like magic. With careful handling, she might land him for her niece yet. The stupid chit must be given time to cool down, however.

"She's feeling less peaky. We'll have a regular lunch sent up for her."

"There are private parlors to be had if you think she'd like to get out and stretch her legs," he tempted.

Such blandishments were easily resisted when it was the niece's company he was after. "No, she'll want to remain with me. I suppose you've inquired after Thomas?"

"He isn't here. I've tried for him by name and by description, and they haven't seen him. There are dozens of other hotels and inns here; he's probably at one closer to the dock. Bournemouth is becoming a bit fashionable. He'd keep a low profile. I have recruited a few helpers to check out other inns, but if all else fails, I'll catch him when he tries to board ship tonight. I'd prefer to get the thing done before dark, if possible. Darkness offers too many chances of a slipup."

"He wouldn't stay at an inn at all if he's wise. Why should he when he has a friend living not two miles away?"

"What!" It was a howl of protest. "Why didn't you tell me? Who is this friend? Where does he live?"

Well experienced in deception, she looked only mildly surprised as she said, "Young Stokely lives just north of here, between Bournemouth and Lymington. You know Everett Stokely."

"No, but I'll find him."

"What helpers have you hired?"

He gave a mocking grin. "I shan't tell you. Your niece wouldn't approve."

"Millie?" she asked. He didn't answer, but not denying it was answer enough. "A wise move! Thomas wouldn't want to be without a woman for long."

His grin faded, and a frown creased his brow. When he

spoke, he lowered his voice. "How could you let her marry a man like that?"

Faith heard the softer sounds and drew nearer to the door to eavesdrop.

"Lud, you sound as though *partis* grew on trees. The more eligible ones are impossible to nab. They're spoken for from the cradle. So many of the second sons are marrying untitled fortunes that it makes hard foraging for gels like Faith who are expected to marry a title but haven't much to barter with."

"The solution seems obvious. They should marry untitled fortunes as well."

He tried to sound casual, but she didn't misread the alert set of his shoulders. To throw a rub in his way and increase his ardor, she said, "It's not so easy as that."

"I know a commoner doesn't automatically assume his lady's title, but . . ."

She bridled up to hear him outline the lack of advantage to himself in this merger. "He makes excellent connections though. What I meant was that the Mordains have *never* married mere gentility. Lady Faith would be the last woman in the world to take a social step downwards."

"I see." Something in his face froze. She felt as if a door had been closed right while she stood talking to him. "She knows what is important to her, of course. If she feels the necessity of mingling more blue blood with hers, then of course my suggestion is ineligible."

They both fell silent. Faith's patience broke, and she walked into the room to learn what was being discussed. Guy lifted his eyes and stared at her. She had never seen such a malevolent gaze. His nostrils were pinched and his lips were drawn into a thin line, but it was his glittering topaz stare that froze her.

"What are you talking about?" Faith demanded.

"About catching Thomas, of course. That's why we're here," Guy reminded her. Her own icy glare froze the blood in his veins. How could a woman be such a fool?

Lady Lynne looked from one to the other and decided it was time to give Mr. Delamar a little encouragement. "I really am astonished that Thomas should be so daring and innovative as to have arranged this business,'' she said. This would give Guy a chance to outline his superior innovation.

He failed her entirely. "It isn't his lack of *morals* that astonishes you?'' he asked.

"That goes without saying,'' Faith rushed in. Guy's slow, mocking grin greeted her words. "That he is *innocent*, I mean!'' she exclaimed angrily.

"You certainly won't hear *me* say anything of the sort,'' he gibed. "I'll leave you ladies now. I have a million things to do. I'll send a waiter up for your order.''

He left, and Faith flounced back to her room, then flounced back again to her aunt. "Are we just going to sit here while he goes and arrests Thomas?''

"Of course not, ninnyhammer!'' The last trace of distress faded from Lady Lynne's face, to be replaced by a lively smile. "We are going to search the hotels and inns and find Thomas, while Guy wastes his time out chasing mares' nests.'' She quickly outlined her maneuver.

It sounded possible of success to Faith, and she went along with it. Of course her aunt had to have a snack before leaving the inn, which wasted nearly an hour. It gave Faith time to consider what she was about to do. Was it morally right to help a criminal escape justice? She knew perfectly well it was not but rationalized that she'd urge Thomas to return all the money. Then it would be all right.

She sat jiggling with impatience while her aunt stolidly ate her way through not only the toast and tea but also a couple of coddled eggs. "Now can we go?'' she asked as the last bit of yolk disappeared.

"Do you know, I am feeling a trifle queasy,'' was Lady Lynne's answer. "Really, I am not feeling at all well,'' she added. One had only to look at her to see that it was true. She looked like a dying camel. She had turned very pale, and her eyes looked rheumy.

"Then I'll go alone,'' Faith said. "With the groom, I mean.''

Much as her chaperone wished to accompany her, it was

impossible. She straggled to her bed and lay down. "Oh, very well. Run along then, but be careful, Faith," she said in a weak voice. Then she pulled the counterpane over her and closed her eyes.

Faith got her bonnet and pelisse and darted downstairs. While she was waiting for the carriage, she saw Delamar enter the lobby. He looked ready for treason. He couldn't be back from the wild-goose chase so soon! But she knew he was, and he knew as well that it had been a hoax. She stood silent, hidden by a potted palm, and watched to see where he went next. He pulled out his watch, glanced at it, then looked around the lobby, obviously expecting to meet someone. Her first fear was that he had laid a plan to ambush Thomas. She watched, her heart in her throat.

In less than two minutes, Guy spotted his quarry and hurried forward. Faith followed him with her eyes and saw not Thomas but Millie, the lightskirt from Fareham. When Guy put out his hand and took Millie by the elbow, some uncontrollable demon entered Faith's soul. She strode forward from behind the concealing palm and accosted him. The angry glow in his eyes incited her to further madness.

"I see I was worried unnecessarily that you'd find Thomas," she sneered. "I made sure the story would take precedence over everything else, even your lechery."

"Congratulations, Lady Faith. You have misjudged my interest like everything else. Don't worry, I'll have his giblets on a platter despite your best efforts to thwart me."

Millie listened eagerly to this exchange. She noticed that Guy was fumbling with his watch. She also noticed that while he continued to ring a peal over the pretty lady about deceiving him, he put his hand on her arm and tried to lead her back upstairs.

"I am appalled that your aunt permitted you out alone in a watering hole like this," he said sternly, and as he held the lady's interest with this charade, he deftly opened her purse and dropped his watch into it. Now what the devil was he up to? Millie wondered.

"It's none of your concern," Lady Faith said loftily.

"And I don't need lessons in propriety from *you*, sir," she added, casting a withering sneer on Millie, who enjoyed the altercation immensely. It was like having a front seat at a play. "I am going for a drive along the promenade in the carriage with the groom."

"Then I shall accompany you to your carriage," he insisted.

"I think not. There is *some* company that is less respectable than a young lady's being alone." On this cutting speech she turned and stalked away.

"Bravo," Millie congratulated her escort. "Where are we off to?"

"The constable's office," he said blandly. "It is shocking that an earl's daughter should steal a gentleman's watch when he is only trying to help her."

"You're never going to have a lady locked up in the roundhouse!" Millie gasped.

"It will keep her out of a worse prison, one that would last the rest of her life," he said grimly. Yet he knew this daring step might kill any chance of forgiveness. He walked to the window and watched for Faith's carriage to emerge from the yard.

"They'll never lock her up," Millie warned. "A warning—that's all the likes of her will get."

"You underestimate me. I don't plan to call just any old constable but Mr. Mather, who owes me a rather large favor."

"Old Jem Mather, the one you helped to catch the smashers." Millie smiled. "You let him take the credit for that when it was you and your lads who found the plates they used for forging money."

"Now you see how my modesty pays off. *I* got the story and let the constables have the honor. There's no money in that."

"She won't really be driving along the promenade," Millie said.

"Very true, but she'll be in the carriage scouting the inns for word of that maw worm she's engaged to. I have to get to the constable's office immediately before we lose her. You see if you can find out what the aunt's up to, Millie. And if she leaves here, follow her."

"I was going to talk to the abbess and see if she's done any business with Lord Thomas," Millie reminded him.

"I'll do that as soon as Lady Faith is under lock and key. You're sure Elwood is at the Exeter Hotel?"

"Calling hisself Mr. James, unless there's two London gents with red hair and freckles hiding in Bournemouth. It's odd the two thieves ain't putting up together."

"Not that odd. There is no honor between this particular pair of thieves."

"Why don't you have Elwood arrested at least?" Millie urged.

"He doesn't have the money, not in his room at any rate. Isn't that what you said?" She nodded. "Besides, if I fail to find Thomas, there's a chance Elwood will succeed. He knows him better than I do and might have some ideas. Tessie is keeping an eye on Elwood, so he won't go far. Meet me back here in, say, an hour if you aren't out following Lady Lynne."

"What if she leads me to this Lord Thomas gent? What do I do?"

"Just keep following them till you can send word back to me. If any of your friends turn up here, you might enlist their aid."

"Us girls don't work the Royal Bath, Guy. The clerk is already giving me funny looks. If I wasn't with you, he'd've showed me the door long ago."

"That's because he don't recognize a *real* lady when he sees one," Guy told her.

"You'll be careful of Lord Thomas," Millie urged with a frown of concern.

"Of course."

"How will you take him?"

"It's like any other maneuver. I'll work out a broad field of vision, a clear field of fire, and make sure I've covered my rear flank."

Faith's carriage came into view, and he hurried out of the hotel to see which way it was going. It turned right, up

Exeter Lane. Her first stop would be the Osborne Hotel, he figured, and if he moved fast, he could have her arrested there. He felt more nervous than when he had faced the enemy in the Peninsula and more determined to succeed.

Chapter Nine

When Lady Faith was attending a seminary for young ladies, she had once accepted an invitation home to tea with the daughter of a social-climbing merchant. She was given to understand by her mama that this had been a grave indiscretion on her part, and it was never to be spoken of in public. Lower than the visit to the mansion of a cit she had never sunk till that day. Nothing prepared her for the indignity of being hauled from her carriage and accompanied, rather roughly, into the local roundhouse.

When first accosted by Constable Mather, she thought for one wild, confused instant that he was a highwayman in the middle of a city and was frightened to death. "Unhand me! Let go at once or I'll call the constable!" she objected.

He had opened the carriage door and entered when the groom slowed down at a corner. While one hand grabbed her reticule, his other hand got hold of her wrist. He growled, "That won't be necessary, miss, I *am* the constable."

She looked into a moon face, fringed with snuff-colored hair, then to the badge of office affixed to his jacket. "But what do you want? What are you doing with my reticule?" she demanded, and tried to get it back.

He lifted it beyond her reach. "Just come along nice and quiet now, and no tricks," Mather said.

"Let me go!" she exclaimed. She tried to fight him off, but he was persistent and very strong for such a pasty-faced man. His fingers bit like claws into her arms, and she was lifted bodily from the banquette. She called to pedestrians passing in the street for help. They sneered and gave encouraging nods to the constable. In their eyes she read the disdain and derision so often mirrored in her own. She might as well have been a pesky dog for all they cared. Her whole world was turned upside down, landing her in a topsy-turvy land where nothing made any sense.

"Step lively now, miss," Mather said, and pulled her to another carriage standing by. He opened the door and shoved her inside. He called her "miss" as though she were a serving wench or worse. He obviously didn't know who she was.

"You are making a mistake, sir," she said with as much dignity as the occasion permitted. "I am Lord Westmore's daughter. My name is Lady Faith Mordain, of Mordain Hall. And if you don't let me go at once, you will be very sorry."

He shook his brindled head and opened her reticule to pull out an object, which he hid in his hand. "Shame on you, melady," he said. " 'Tis bad enough when the muslin company snaffles a gent's watch, but for a fine lady like yourself to sink so low . . . You ought to be made an example of." From his fingers dangled Mr. Delamar's gold timepiece. There was no mistaking the engraving on its lid or the twisted piece of metal that was the remains of a spent bullet.

Her eyes grew large with confused consternation. "How did that get there?"

"You tell me, and we'll both know," Mather said wisely.

Shock and confusion slowed her brain, but the truth soon became clear to her. "This is Delamar's work!" She gasped. How had the constable known the watch was in her reticule if Mr. Delamar hadn't told him? And how had Delamar known if he hadn't put it there himself? "He put it there himself!" she announced.

"Surely he did. That's why he reported it stolen, no doubt."

"I knew it! He sent you after me!"

"That he did not, miss. He only reported it stolen. It was the clerk at the Royal Bath as saw you snaffle the bit. Your fine da will do you no good now, melady."

The carriage pulled into a side street and stopped at the roundhouse. It was a small stone edifice, and as she was dragged along the path to it, Faith noticed the bars on the windows. From one of the windows a man's face leered at her. She had never seen such an ugly specimen of humankind in her life. He looked more like an animal than a human being. A growing horror dried up her protests. Was she going to be put into a cell, locked up like a felon?

Officer Mather did not lead her to a cell, not immediately at least. He took her to his own office and pointed at the chair behind the desk, the only chair in the room. "I'll just send notice to Mr. Delamar that you've been apprehended," he announced smugly. "It will be for him to decide what becomes of you."

"Don't bother," she said.

"You admit you took it, then?"

Anger welled up, giving her courage. "Certainly not, but he will *say* I did. He put it in my purse himself, I tell you." She looked around the airless, shabby room. Hope shrank to resignation that this would take some time to clear up. "Well, what are you going to do with me?"

"You just set yourself down and behave." Mather knew he was doing wrong and felt a twinge as Lady Faith's noble eyes pierced him, memorizing every line of his face, for future vengeance no doubt.

"If you know any solicitors, sir," she said haughtily, "I suggest you get in touch with one without delay. Meanwhile, you will notify my aunt, Lady Lynne, at the Royal Bath Hotel that I have been wrongfully incarcerated. And you had better do it if you value your hide," she added coldly.

Guy had given him no instructions in that regard, but a prisoner *did* have the right to notify her family. With such a quantity of noble names being sprinkled over the constable's head, he deemed it wise to deviate as little as possible from the written laws.

"She'll be notified, never you fear," he assured her. He went out and locked the door behind him. His most urgent wish was to speak to Guy Delamar, but as he had no notion in the world where to find him, he sent a minion off to the Royal Bath Hotel with two messages; one for Lady Lynne, the other a call for help to Guy. This done, he sat trembling in his boots at what form Lady Lynne might take.

At that moment, Lady Lynne was just pulling herself up from her bed. A short rest had restored her health, her curiosity, and her desire to recover her money. She regretted that Faith had taken the carriage, but the Pleasure Gardens were just across the road. She would take a stroll there and keep an eye on the road for Faith's return.

A stroll in a public garden was an unexceptionable place to meet unattached gentlemen, so she made a careful toilette. When she went downstairs, she wore a charming straw bonnet trimmed with cherries and black grapes that looked so real they made her hungry. She strode forth, looking sharply about for acquaintances of either sex. The patrons of the Royal Bath were members of the ton—trust Guy to put them up at the very best establishment. She recognized a few faces but no names. It occurred to her that the registry would tell her whether any of her bosom beaux were here, so she went to the front desk.

There was a man in front of her speaking to the clerk. He was a tall, gangly drink of water, with red hair. He looked a rung lower than most of the customers, so she paid little heed to him till he spoke. Then her ears perked up and she moved closer to hear the conversation. It nearly knocked her base over apex for joy.

"I don't suppose you have a Lord Thomas Vane putting up here?" the man asked.

The clerk shook his head. "You're the second one looking for him. No, he's not here. Sorry."

"He might be using another name. He's a tall, handsome fellow. About my age, with black hair. He'd have come in a yellow curricle."

"Lots of gents come in yellow curricles this time of year. Leave your name if you like, and I'll tell him you called."

"No!" the man said swiftly. "No, don't tell him. But if he comes, would you have a message sent off to me at this address?" He took a piece of paper and scribbled something on it.

Lady Lynne stood, transfixed with interest. Was it Mr. Elwood? Surely it was. Someone had mentioned his red hair.

"Excuse me," she said, and pulled at his elbow. "I heard you asking for Lord Thomas Vane. I'm on the same errand myself. You must be Mr. Elwood, I think?"

"Eh?" The man turned a ruddy, angry face toward her. "No, my name's Jones."

She shot a sapient glance at him. "And mine's Queen Charlotte!" she shot back. "You're Elwood, and if you don't want me to raise a ruckus, you'd better have a word with me. Come along."

She took him by the arm and drew him aside toward a brace of chairs in the lobby. The man went reluctantly, but he went. "Who are you?" he asked, his voice surly.

"One of your victims! That's enough for you to know. I could land you in jail this instant, so we'll have no monkey business, my good man. Now, I take it Thomas tipped you the double?"

"That he did!" the man admitted.

"Then you are Elwood."

"What if I am?"

"Did Thomas skip with all the money?"

"Every last penny of it."

"Have you any notion where he's gone?"

"To France—that's where we were both heading. We were supposed to be leaving next week."

110

"What makes you think he's in Bournemouth?"

"I had a word with our travel agent," he said, clenching his fist to show the physical nature of their discussion. "He's here somewhere, and I mean to find him."

She regarded him silently for a moment and decided he was telling the truth. Furthermore, their aims were not inimical. "We'll work together," she decided.

"What do you know about all this?" he asked, and looked at her with growing interest.

"I know Guy Delamar is out scouring the town looking for you both."

"Delamar! He's the cause of it all! It was his article that set Thomas off."

"Don't be an idiot. The reason he wrote that story is because he learned somehow that Thomas meant to flit."

"How could he know?"

"How should *I* know? He has spies all over town reporting to him. He was suspicious of the Afro-Gold company, I expect, and put out a few spies to sniff around."

"Where is Delamar?" Elwood asked.

"I've taken care of him—for the moment. He's off on a wild-goose chase, which gives us a while to find Thomas."

"Damme, I've been looking since yesterday. I've been to every inn and hotel and tourist haunt in town. It begins to look as though he's not here at all. I think the demmed travel agent led me astray."

"That's possible, and if it's true, then we're both out of our money. On the other hand, he may be here. Delamar says he booked passage on a ship leaving tonight."

"I can't help you," Elwood said. "I wager if Thomas is here, the Bloodhound of Fleet Street will find him for us."

"I am counting on it," she agreed pleasantly.

"Then what do you want *me* for?"

"To knock Delamar on the head when he finds Thomas and give us time to get our money," she answered frankly. "I get first kick at the cat. He has five thousand guineas of mine and I mean to have it back. If you know what's good for you, you'll return the rest to the rightful owners. But that is entirely up to you," she added enticingly.

Elwood studied her and did some rapid figuring. The five-thousand-guinea investment rang a bell. "You're Lady Faith's aunt!" he said.

"What if I am?"

"I see." He nodded his head and continued thinking. It was soon clear to him that the lady cared not a fig for Lord Thomas but was interested in recovering her money and keeping the whole matter quiet for her charge's sake. Further consideration showed him that she could hardly report the matter as she had chosen to involve herself in it. She wouldn't announce to the world that she had arranged for him to steal the money, and therefore no one would be the wiser. Thomas, the villain, would hardly dare to return to polite society. A sly smile settled on his freckled face. "I don't see why we can't work together. You just let me know when Delamar returns and I'll be after him like a shadow."

"Where will you be? I may have to get in touch with you in a hurry."

"Right here. I'll move into the Royal Bath."

"Fine. You'd best book a room now and keep to it, for Delamar will recognize you. I'll tell you when he arrives. Have a footman bring your things from wherever you're staying. This is no time to leave. Delamar might be back at any moment."

They rose and strolled together to the registration desk. It was again a Mr. James who registered, and a certain Tessie Clements who made note of it. Millie had already been hinted out of the lobby by the clerk and was forced to stroll up and down outside the hotel. Tessie ran to relay her news.

Both girls recognized Jem Mather's minion when he hastened into the hotel. He had often escorted them to the roundhouse. "You'll have to go in and see what he's up to,'' Millie said. ''They've already invited me to leave.''

Tessie saw the minion go to the desk, watched and listened as he was directed to Lady Lynne, and heard her outrage when she read the note. ''It's impossible! They've locked up my niece, Lady Faith!'' she exclaimed.

Elwood grabbed the note and scanned it. He could see no immediate way in which this could be put to his advantage, but Lady Lynne soon realized that her companion could save her a trip to the roundhouse, which was bound to be extremely unpleasant. ''You'll have to go and rescue her,'' she informed him.

''But why would they have locked her up?'' he asked, totally confused.

''No reason is given. It is obviously a mistake. Ring a loud peal over them, and they'll let her free. I'll stay here and keep an eye out for Delamar's return.''

Elwood pretended to agree to this course as it allowed him to escape the old harpy. He left the hotel but only to speak to his groom. ''I've got a possible line on Thomas,'' he said. ''Do you know what Guy Delamar looks like?''

''Yes, like an Indian.''

''That's him. I'll be down on the promenade. When Delamar shows up, go to the railing and wave your hand. I'll keep an eye peeled for your signal.''

''Is the Bloodhound after us?'' the groom asked. The expression in his eyes was not quite terror, but it tended in that direction.

''Not *us*, Lord Thomas, but he must know we're involved. I'd as lief not deal with Delamar.''

''Crikey, me neither.''

''Wave your handkerchief, and when I've seen your signal, I'll wave back.''

Mr. Elwood hurried down to the promenade, looking over his shoulder and all around as he went. He was rapidly reshuffling his plans. If Delamar had got this close to Thomas, then he'd find him, no doubt of that. All he had to do was wait and follow Delamar. He'd take the bossy dame's advice—to a point. No reason he had to give her anything. He'd registered at the Royal Bath under an alias. He'd never remove his things from the Exeter and they'd have no way of tracing him.

Chapter Ten

Bournemouth, though growing, was not yet so large that it had a plethora of abbesses. The abbess of Cranborne was the best known and the likeliest for a visitor to patronize. Her title derived from her establishment on Cranborne Road opposite the Winter Gardens. It was convenient to the Maze, the West Cliff, and both major roads entering the city. Lord Thomas was a notable womanizer, and as the hotels had turned up no clue, Guy hoped the abbess might be able to help him.

The abbess, known as Maggie to her *intimes*, cast a discerning eye over Mr. Delamar and invited him into her private office. "What can I do for you, Mr. Smith?" she inquired. Her gentlemen came in two varieties: Mr. Smith and Mr. Jones.

Abbesses, it seemed to Guy, came in only one form: aging, crafty females of faded beauty. They were usually superannuated lightskirts clever enough to have realized the profit in running an establishment instead of working in one. This one was a dark-eyed brunette nearly as stout as Lady Lynne. On her person she wore a fortune in ugly jewelry and a gown of crimson silk, in the middle of the afternoon.

"I'm looking for Lord Thomas Vane. I've been told you might have done business with him recently."

"Not me. I hardly ever— Ah, yes. He might have come to my establishment, you mean. We entertain a great

115

many gentlemen. I don't seem to recall a Lord Vane in particular . . .''

He knew the best aid to memory and pulled out his money purse. "A tall, handsome fellow. Early thirties, black hair." As he spoke, bills were deposited on her desk, one for each item of description.

She counted the take and said, "He begins to sound familiar. Could you tell me anything else? Another detail or two.''

"Driving a yellow curricle," he said, and placed another bill on the pile. "He'd have come alone, I expect." No sooner was the last bill in place than Maggie's flashing fingers scooped up the pile and deposited it in her bodice.

"He used Belle. I'll call her." She went to the door and hollered.

A young female soon joined them. She didn't look a day over sixteen, but already her face wore the harried look of dissipation. She also looked rather stupid. She ran her eyes over Guy and smiled a wan enticement. "Come on, this way," she said.

"The gentleman only wants to talk, Belle," Maggie said.

"What?''

"About the Mr. Smith you entertained last night. Tell him what you know.''

Belle wasn't much accustomed to talking. "He was all right. Nothing queer in him," she offered.

"Did he happen to mention where he is staying?" Guy asked.

"No, they don't usually.''

"Anything at all that might have given you an idea? Did he mention the water, the Bowling Green, the Maze—anything at all?''

She frowned and bit her thumb. "Bells . . . something about bells," she said vaguely.

"A church, perhaps?" he asked, looking to Maggie for help. "Trinity Church?''

Maggie frowned and shook her head. "He came in from

116

the west—he mentioned something about a cart overturned on Poole Hill Road. What church would that be? St. Michael's!'' she exclaimed. ''There's a new row of flats across the street from it. They're taking tourists to fill up the rooms till they get permanent tenants.''

A grin split Guy's face. ''How do I get there?''

''Turn right at the corner, up Tregonwell, and left at Poole Hill Road. You can't miss the flats—they're new and right across from the church.''

''Just one more thing: Did Mr. Smith happen to mention his real name, Belle?''

''No, they don't,'' she told him.

Maggie, more alert, smelled trouble. ''Is Lord Vane traveling under an alias? What has he done, eh?''

''That's what I'm trying to find out,'' Guy said vaguely. He gave Belle a tip, then left. Maggie, in a fit of generosity, said to Belle, ''Keep it.''

''Thank you ever so! That's the easiest blunt I ever made.''

''Let's hope he comes back,'' Maggie replied. Not that she'd give him that idiot of a Belle. Millie, now, would suit him better.

Guy drove immediately to the flats across from St. Michael's Church. A discreet sign in the window of the end flat announced ''Office.'' He made his inquiries and was told a gentleman fitting the given description had hired a room but had never occupied it. ''An elderly man was in once or twice—a retainer, no doubt. The tenant just took in his luggage and left. I haven't seen him since.''

''Which flat?'' Guy asked.

''Top floor, corner rooms of the east end facing the street, but you won't find him there.''

''I'll have a look all the same. Perhaps you'd come with me and open the door. I'd like to leave a message.''

''You can slide a note under the door. He's not there, and he was very particular about me not letting anybody in. What's the lad done, eh?'' he asked wisely. ''Something he shouldn't, I warrant, but he didn't do it here.''

''Read it in the next issue of the *Harbinger*.''

Guy returned to his carriage and sat thinking. Lord Thomas was cagier than he had thought. He had taken the precaution of depositing the money in the flat with a man to guard it while he himself put up elsewhere. If he were caught, there'd be no evidence on him. He could bring a constable and pick up the money now, then have Thomas arrested when he came to collect it. That was the sane thing to do. What was preventing him?

In his mind, a pair of cool gray eyes pleaded silently. They'd be shooting fireworks at this moment, behind the walls of the roundhouse. Not that it would do her any harm to be brought down a peg! Having her arrested was harsh, but he really couldn't have the ladies interfering with his work, leading him on more bootless errands while they found Thomas. That was his thanks for bringing them along. He never should have permitted it. Why had he? As if he didn't know. From the first moment that proud beauty had sneered down her patrician nose at him, he had been lost.

Lady Lynne was safely incapacitated, but Faith was so sure her noble Thomas was a saint that she might involve herself in the fray. How could he cure her of that infatuation? There'd be the devil to pay after having locked her up. Perhaps if he handled Thomas's arrest with kid gloves, showed her he wasn't completely heartless . . .

He wondered what time it was. He missed his watch. Thomas's ship was scheduled to leave at nine. He'd be back by eight to collect his money. Could he leave Faith locked up with thieves and worse that long? Could the foolish aunt be depended on to keep her out of mischief if he got her out of the roundhouse now? He'd go and get Faith set free, have a good, long talk with her. When she learned that Thomas was really guilty, she'd feel differently. She'd thank him. He pulled the check string and directed his groom to Mather's office.

Two hours had passed since her arrest, and the intervening interval had done nothing to assuage her temper. Why didn't someone come? Why hadn't her aunt come to bail her out? No one but a fiend would have a lady locked up; no one but a devil would trump up a false charge against her. Why had he done it? As her temper mounted, Faith was quite convinced that Mr. Delamar was an agent of Satan. She wouldn't be a bit surprised if he meant to falsify charges against Thomas as well just to get a good story!

Poor Officer Mather was nearly as distraught as she. To have a lady arrested for five minutes for a prank was one thing. He thought Guy would be there to set her free and talk her around to smiles. And the aunt—why hadn't she come? He even went so far as to suggest to Lady Faith that he would send for a solicitor for her if she liked.

"No, thank you, but I suggest *you* hire one for yourself," she replied, cold as an icicle.

Losing his position was the best he could hope for. If the nobility took it into its head to harass him, he was done for. He'd pack up and go to America, if he ever got out of Newgate. He leaped at Delamar like a wild dog when he came into the roundhouse.

"Where the deuce have you been? She's going to sic her solicitor on me! I'll end up doing the hangman's jig."

"Nonsense. Your duty is to maintain law and order. My watch was stolen; you arrested the thief. You did the right thing, Jem."

"It feels mighty like the wrong thing to me! And the young lady says she didn't steal it, either."

"How did she take her arrest?"

"Like a lady, squalling and protesting to beat the devil. Are you going in there?" he asked skeptically.

"Yes, I'd like a word with the prisoner, if you please."

"You'd best take a whip with you. She'll scratch your eyes out."

"It won't be the first time," Guy answered airily.

Mather unlocked the door and drew as far away from it as he could get, which was not all that far. The entire roundhouse was no bigger than a pantry.

Faith heard the key in the lock and jumped up from the chair. She expected to see her aunt and was ready to give her a tongue-lashing for the long delay in rescuing her.

When she saw Mr. Delamar's yellow eyes staring at her, she turned a deathly, furious shade of white.

He took a step toward her, hands extended in peace. "Faith, I want to . . ."

She drew back, perfectly rigid. She looked at her caller as though he were a dead rat. "There is no need to explain, Mr. Delamar. I have had ample time to figure out your scheme. You put your watch in my reticule on purpose to allow your cohort to arrest me. That is entrapment—or worse—and it will be reported as such as soon as I am free."

The unlocked door beckoned. She strode toward it, whisking past Guy and lifting her skirts as though to avoid contamination. His hand shot out and grabbed her arm.

"Not so fast! You're still under arrest, and Officer Mather has the evidence to prove you guilty."

"You know perfectly well I didn't steal your watch!"

"The clerk at the hotel says otherwise. I am shocked at you, Faith," he said, attempting to lighten the mood.

She tried to shake off his hand, but he only took hold of her other arm as well, to compound the offense. "How dare you touch me!" she demanded. Her nostrils quivered in disgust, and her gray eyes flared.

His ire rose up to meet the challenge from this haughty beauty. *Dare* to *touch* her, indeed, as though she were sanctified by her blue blood! "I'm not fussy," he sneered.

"So I have noticed. If you have any hope of climbing the ladder to respectability, I recommend you *become* fussy—if you are able to discriminate between lightskirts and ladies, that is to say."

"It's easy. Lightskirts are a deal prettier and usually more polite as well."

"If the refined manners of a Millie are what appeals to you, then, of course, you are wise to stick to your own kind."

He released her arms and stared balefully at her. "I've seen more real manners from Millie and her sisters these past two days than during my entire acquaintance with you and your aunt. You don't mind using my brains and my

120

connections and my wallet so long as I keep my head bowed and tug my forelock every second minute. And, of course, refrain from *touching* your noble bodies."

"One must draw the line somewhere," she snipped, with a toss of her shoulders. "Don't worry, you'll be repaid as soon as we get back to London."

"I doubt that very much."

"Are you calling me a liar?"

A cold sneer settled on his face. " 'A very honest woman—but something given to lie,' as the redoubtable Mr. Shakespeare so wisely said."

Her hand rose and whipped across his face with all the force she possessed. The echo of the slap reverberated in the silent room. It had the effect of removing his hateful sneer, only to replace it with a blazing anger. Faith watched, aghast at what her temper had led her into, while Mr. Delamar stared with wildly dilated eyes and the imprint of her hand turned to rose on his cheek. When his hands came out, she thought he was going to strike her or shake her. He almost thought so himself.

It wasn't till he touched her and saw the fear in her eyes that he knew what would be a worse punishment—to treat her like the lightskirts she despised. His fingers tightened ruthlessly as he pulled her into his arms. The odd and startling thing was that she didn't resist. Perhaps she considered a struggle beneath her dignity, which served to heighten his wrath.

As his face descended to hers, she looked up, wide-eyed, at him. "What are you—" she whispered breathlessly. Before she could finish the question, she was crushed against his hard body and his lips were bruising hers with a fiercely punishing kiss. There was no tenderness now, no gentleness, but the wild ravening of the unleashed tiger. She was stunned into frightened acquiescence at first, but when his hand moved over her back, pulling her closer till she could feel the buttons of his jacket through her cotton gown, something of the untamed animal stirred in her own breast. A primal force was unleashed, obliterating common sense. She made one weak effort at staving him off, but as her arms rose from her sides, they went involuntarily around his neck, tentatively at first, but soon tightening as her blood quickened to his rhythm and the increasing pressure of his lips. It was a moment of desperate frustration, when she knew she should be outraged but could only go on clinging to him as if her life depended on it. His lips moved hungrily, arousing dangerous, unknown sensations. Yet hadn't she imagined something like this ever since she had first seen him? Hadn't she wondered what it would be like to be in his arms? Her wildest imagining had never soared this high—she felt heady with power, intoxicated, as if she could rule the world. But she wanted only to rule this man, whose hot kisses drove her to ecstasy. She felt his body suddenly quiver, then stiffen. He pulled away swiftly, leaving her in a state of emotional chaos. He actually pushed her from him and regarded her with contempt. It was the last thing she expected.

In confusion, she asked, "Why did you do that?"

"I've just been asking myself the same thing about your sudden warmth. It wouldn't have anything to do with Thomas, would it? Exerting your feminine guiles on his behalf? Give the commoner a taste of the real stuff and he'll do your bidding? I'm not so easily gulled as Willie Shaft."

"No!"

"I understand your reasoning."

She stared at him silently while trying to make sense of this charge. It had all been some sort of stunt. Pride came to her rescue. Her passions were directed in a new course, lending heat to her reply. "And I understand yours. You'd do anything to persecute Thomas, wouldn't you? You're afraid I'll convince him to return the money—if he ever took it in the first place! That would make dull reading, indeed! Nobleman *not* guilty in fraud scheme! Much livelier muckraking to blazon his guilt across the banner. Why, I shouldn't be surprised if you sell an extra dozen subscriptions. You might even be able to afford two rooms instead of that small pig sty you usually wallow in."

Her words, so adamant and insulting and angry, showed

122

him his case was hopeless. Any hope of pacification was at an end, and frustration turned his neck red. "I wonder where you'd be today if you hadn't been born with a silver spoon in your craw. It's easy to look down your patrician nose at me. At least I pay for my own pig sty by the sweat of my brow and not by stealing from honest men."

"The sweat of your brow?" She emitted a high, ironic laugh. "The sweat of your common, twisted mind is more like it. You'd be less contemptible if you dug ditches. You planted evidence to have me arrested, and I wouldn't be a bit surprised if you mean to do the same to Thomas. At least you've the low cunning to realize the profit in writing about your *betters*."

His voice took on a new, menacing tone as his yellow eyes narrowed. "Don't goad me too far, milady. There's more than one noble scoundrel involved in this affair now. 'Lady Faith Mordain Arrested as Accessory' would amuse Mam'selle Ondit's readers."

"You go beyond my worst opinion of you. You achieve depths I could never have imagined. I knew you were low, but till this minute I had no idea how low and disgusting a man can be. I can hardly credit that I once admired you. Yes, you may well stare. You waste your talents, sir. You ought to be on the stage, ranting of honest reporting and the duty of a journalist to right the wrongs of society. *Hypocrite!*" She spat the word at him.

"I have no intentions of printing that! I was just . . . Dammit, Faith . . ."

Tears stung her eyes, and she blinked them away. The lump in her throat made further words impossible. She clenched her hands into balls in an effort to control her emotions. Delamar stood uncertainly, still hoping to conciliate her.

"I just wanted to keep you clear when the dirt flies," he said, not quite truthfully.

"Have you had Thomas arrested?" she asked. Her voice was flintlike, the only tone possible to her if she was to speak at all.

"It will happen within the next few hours."

"What have you learned?"

"I know where he'll be and where he has the money. Elwood isn't with him. He robbed Elwood as well. Noble behavior, indeed! But then we must remember his origins," he said sardonically.

She swallowed down her hot retort. "Where is he?"

"It doesn't matter. *I* know where he is."

"You must tell me!"

"I think not. You'd spoil the story," he said, and turned to leave the room.

"Wait! You can't leave me here!"

"Can't?" he asked, and looked at her for a long moment. "I don't see why not." He opened the door and said in a loud voice to Mather, "Book her, Officer. I'll lay charges now."

Mather stared at him as though the world had gone mad. "Eh? You mean write it up in my book?"

"Whatever the normal procedure is, follow it." He scribbled his name on the sheet, stalked from the round-house, hopped into his carriage, and returned to the Royal Bath Hotel. Faith's insults rang in his ears, raising his anger to such heights that he didn't regret his rash acts for several blocks. Accusing him of exploiting his *betters* and wallowing in a pig sty was bad enough, but it was the slur on his journalistic integrity that cut the deepest. To accuse him of setting Thomas up for the sake of a story was unforgivable. He was tempted to print the news of her arrest, but discretion hadn't abandoned him entirely. That was going too far, given the circumstances.

He should go back now and have Mather free her, but she might find her way to Thomas and undo his work. She still loved Thomas, that was obvious. But for one wild, unbelievable moment it tasted like she loved him. There was passion lurking there—why couldn't there be any common sense? A blind, foolish girl fascinated by Thomas Vane's handsome looks—that was what it amounted to. She didn't know, or care, a thing about his character. Yet she had said she had admired him before . . . He had begun to wedge his way into her affections, but it was hopeless now. He'd take a constable to the flats on Poole Hill Road and arrest Lord Thomas Vane. At least Eddie and Buck would get their money back—and the others, too, of course. Lady Lynne would recover her five thousand guineas. Perhaps Lady Lynne would put in a good word for him with Faith . . .

He shook himself back to reality when he realized what he was thinking. He never gave up: that was his strength, and his weakness. He always assessed his tools and talents, then determined how to do the job that needed doing. It had served him well in war, but in love . . . Why not? All's fair in love and war. He could . . . No, some courses were too rough for civilians. It would be unfair to take the money from the flat and plant it on Elwood, to say Thomas had only gone after him to recover the funds. Besides, it would leave Lord Thomas smelling of roses and free to return to Faith. Recover the money and let Thomas go free? It would give Eddie and Buck and the others their money back, but it would rob him of his journalistic coup. And it would still not publicly disgrace Thomas. The wedding might still go forth.

He had to make Faith realize that Thomas was a bounder and a thief and that he himself was not so low as she thought. He wasn't *just* after the story at any cost. What if he captured Thomas and the money privately without bringing in the police? She and Thomas would be spared public disgrace, but it would be acknowledged privately that Thomas was slime. Surely she wouldn't marry him after that. She couldn't be that madly in love. What would Thomas do then? Enough people would know the truth so that he couldn't return to society. Lady Lynne, for instance, wouldn't keep her tongue between her teeth forever. He'd disappear to America or France or wherever he felt the life would suit him. A pity to turn him loose on some other society, but the world contained many such creatures and folks must constantly be on their guard.

That was it, then. He'd capture Thomas and send him packing. Once he was gone, he'd try to repair the damage done between Faith and himself. Elwood's freedom was thrown in as an afterthought. He could hardly arrest the man when he wasn't the one who ran off with the money, even if he'd intended to do so.

Guy went to his room and took a pistol from his valise. As he was leaving the hotel, he met Millie and Tessie loitering in the street. They eagerly pointed out that Mr. Elwood was hanging around the promenade.

"That guy up on the balcony waved a hanky at him when you went in," Millie added. "A signal for him to follow you, likely."

"That's just what I don't need. Tessie, you get into my rig. Quick, before he sees who enters. Keep your head clear of the window. Better yet, tuck your hair up under this," he said, and handed her his hat. "Have my groom drive you around for a couple of hours—out in the country, I think. That will draw Elwood off. Lead Elwood back here later. I'll want a word with him."

"What do *I* do?" Millie asked eagerly.

"Stay here and keep an eye on Lady Lynne. Has she left her room?"

"She might've done that, but she didn't leave the hotel. They put me and Tessie out long ago."

"Do you think you could stop her if she came out?"

"I don't know that I could, not in broad daylight," Millie opined. "Unless, I bashed her over the head and hog-tied her."

He gave a rueful laugh. "That won't be necessary. Tell her—no, don't bother. If she goes anywhere, it will be to the roundhouse. She can't do much damage there except to Mather."

"Where are you going?"

"I've found out where Vane has the blunt. He won't leave without it. I'll be waiting for him."

"How did you find out?" Millie asked.

"Your employer and a girl called Belle told me."

"That Belle is a moonling, I swear."

"Yes, but Maggie is sharp as a razor. She's the one who figured it out."

He waited till his carriage, with Tessie wearing his hat,

had driven off at a fast clip heading west on the Bath Road. In a few minutes, Mr. Elwood's rig followed it. Guy hailed a passing hackney and directed the driver to Poole Road.

In her chamber, Lady Lynne's patience had come to an end. She had given up hanging around the lobby an hour ago. What was the point? Guy would come to her when he returned. What could possibly be taking Mr. Elwood two hours to fetch Faith home? Either the man was incompetent or he was running some new rig. There was nothing for it but to go after the chit herself. And she didn't even have her carriage. She'd have to go in a hired cab.

Before leaving the hotel, she sent a boy up to Mr. Elwood's room with a note on the off chance that he was there. She was told that Mr. Elwood had not taken occupation of his chamber yet. This gave rise to a hope that he had spotted Guy and followed him. That would account for his tardiness in not fetching Faith. It restored her humor somewhat as she was jostled along the busy street to the roundhouse.

Millie watched uncertainly as Lady Lynne left, then decided she'd best hop into a hackney and follow her to be certain she went where Guy said she would. And on top of it all, it was getting late. She and Tessie needed to be back at the abbey by six-thirty for work.

Chapter Eleven

Officer Mather, already sick with regret at what he had done, was ready to embrace Lady Lynne as a savior when she arrived at his door with fire in her eyes and brimstone in her speech. Devilish though she looked, to him she was an angel of mercy. If only he could propitiate her, he might squeak through this imbroglio with his skin intact.

She cast one withering glance at his ignoble premises and demanded, ''Who is in charge of this hovel?''

Mather stepped forward manfully. ''I have the honor, madam. That is—I—me. I am responsible. I did it, but it's all Delamar's fault, I swear an affeydavey.''

Though truculent, Lady Lynne was by no means sure of success in her endeavor. She was more relieved than propitiated by Mather's manner, the word *fault* in particular encouraged her. ''Where is Lady Faith Mordain?''

''She wouldn't have a solicitor. I offered to get her one myself.''

''Bring her out,'' Lady Lynne commanded.

''That I will. Not to say that she'll come—an uncommonly determined young lady, if I may be so bold.''

''No, you may not. What charge is laid against her?''

''It's the watch, you see. The one she stole—took—borrowed—er, *has* that belongs to Mr. Delamar. He's the one laid the charge against her.''

''What, Lady Faith has Delamar's watch?'' she asked in confusion. ''Where the deuce did she get it?''

''From his pocket, he says. He insisted I arrest her.''

"You're an idiot. You have certainly misunderstood Mr. Delamar's instructions. Why, the two of them are close as inkle weavers."

"More like Punch and Judy, it sounded like to me."

The matter became more confusing by the moment. "Has Delamar been here? Has he been talking to her?"

"You might call it talking. A shouting and screaming match is what it was. Aye, and a blow or two exchanged as well, it sounded like. He stormed out of here madder than when he come in. 'Book her,' he says. Book her I did."

"Then you must unbook her immediately and expunge her name from your list of felons. I will not have my niece's name listed in a book with thieves."

"Do you have a solicitor at all?" Mather inquired doubtfully. He liked to be told what to do by persons with some authority. A lady was intimidating, but she made a poor witness in court.

"Unlock that door this instant or I shall bring a magistrate down on your head, you stupid little man."

It was a hard decision. Prisoners were not allowed to walk free, but this prisoner was patently innocent and, worse, a lady. "If you'd care to deposit bail . . ." he suggested.

"How much?"

"A shilling," he said, to ensure acceptance.

Lady Lynne tossed a shilling at his feet, and he scampered forward to unlock the door. Faith had overheard every word and stood ready to leave.

She directed a stern look at Mather and said, "You have not heard the last of this, sir."

His shoulders fell, and he muttered to himself, "Don't I know it."

He watched as the ladies went to their carriage and were driven away. He wondered what that saucy piece of a Millie was doing, following them. Guy was running one of his rigs certainly, and he was glad he was out of it. Then he pocketed his shilling and went to vent his ill humor on his other felons.

Lady Lynne's manner became more friendly when the ladies were alone. "Poor girl," she said, taking Faith's hand to comfort her. "Are you able to tell me how a simple trip to a few hotels to look for Thomas landed you in jail?"

At the first word of sympathy, tears oozed out of Faith's eyes and she collapsed on her aunt's shoulder. In bits and pieces, the story came out, very jumbled and very emotional. "He called me a bounder and says he will print in the *Harbinger* that I was arrested."

"I hope you didn't take that sitting down!"

"Oh, no! I called him worse. I don't know what all I said," she replied, but remembered a few of her choicer insults, every one of which brought forth another tear or hiccough.

"I really do not understand Guy," the aunt admitted. "He has a very odd kick in his gallop. Why would he subject you to such an indignity? I hope—Faith, I hope you did not steal his watch!"

"He put it in my reticule himself. He was angry because I caught him with Millie in the lobby."

"I daresay it has something to do with Thomas, if the truth were known," Lady Lynne said. "He was upset, no doubt, about that little wild-goose chase I sent him on. He was afraid you'd find Thomas and warn him. We must get busy . . ."

Faith turned a startled face to her aunt. "Delamar has already found him. Did I not tell you?"

"Found him! You never mean it! Why didn't you tell me! Where is he?"

Faith explained what she had learned, and her aunt filled her in on the strange appearance and disappearance of Mr. Elwood. As they talked, Lady Lynne noticed that concern for Thomas had taken second place to vexation with Guy Delamar. What a troublesome gel Faith was turning out to be. Bringing Emily and her viscount to terms had been a holiday compared to handling this chit.

Faith noticed that the carriage was returning to the hotel. "What should we do now?" she asked.

"I don't know about you, but I intend to have a stroll

in the Pleasure Gardens. This whole matter has gone beyond my grasp. No matter. Guy will certainly get my money back, but I cannot help regretting that Thomas must be exposed and your skirts splattered with the filth as well. Pity.''

Faith drew a deep sigh. "As much as I despise Mr. Delamar and everything he stands for, he is at least right about Thomas. He had every advantage. There was no excuse for him to do what he did. Stealing from innocent people, and people who needed their bit of money, too.''

"It is kind of you to worry about me," Lady Lynne said.

Faith blinked at such colossal insensitivity. "You, of course, Auntie, and others who are much worse off. Some friends of Mr. Delamar put all they had into the fund. That is why he is so determined to catch Thomas. I begin to regret some of the harsh things I said to him. My temper, alas!''

Faith had no more temper than a teapot. Her coolness was considered her greatest virtue, but at that moment the carriage reached the hotel and Lady Lynne was thinking of something else.

"Who is in that hackney behind us, Faith? I swear it followed me when I left; it was at the roundhouse, and now here it is, still on our heels. Good God, it couldn't be Thomas, seeking our help!''

The look in Faith's eyes had nothing of hope or joy in it. Fear and anger were more like it. The ladies entered the hotel, taking peeps over their shoulders to see who followed them.

"That's Millie, the lightskirt who was at the dock with Guy this morning," Lady Lynne exclaimed. "He was hiring her to help him find Thomas and not to warm his bed as we thought. There's something havey-cavey afoot her, Faith. I'll have a word with her.''

Faith so far forgot propriety as to accompany her aunt back out to the street to accost Millie. The wench ran back to the carriage when she saw what was happening, but she was no match for Lady Lynne. The dame let out a bellow that would have deafened a sergeant major, and a very reluctant Millie came forward.

"Why are you following us?" Lady Lynne asked imperiously.

"To see where you were going, mum."

"Brilliant. Did Delamar put you up to it?"

"Oh, no, mum!"

The dame got a tight grip on the girl's elbow and entered the carriage with her, for she had no desire to be seen on the street in such low company. Faith followed them in. "Now see here, miss, I didn't come down in the last rain. I recognize the fine hand of Delamar at work here, and you'll sit in this rig till you tell me what you know."

"I don't know nothing. I've got to go to work."

"Not one step till you open your budget. And if you don't, I'll have you delivered promptly to the roundhouse."

Millie cast a sly smile at Faith. "I wager there's a cell free right about now."

Lady Lynne's eyes narrowed and she turned to her niece. "She's in on the whole affair, you see."

"She was with Guy when he put his watch in my reticule," Faith pointed out.

"Aha! Collusion in a fraud! Direct the driver to the roundhouse, Faith."

"I've got to go to work!" Millie howled.

"Your *regular* line of work is also against the law, if you don't know it already," Lady Lynne added in her most threatening voice.

Millie shook her head in resignation. "Well, if you two ain't a pair of sapskulls. You'd think you'd be happy to set back and let Guy look after you. He's only trying to get your money back, milady," she said to the elder. Then she turned a pair of dancing black eyes on the younger. "And he was afraid you'd whiddle the whole scrap to that Lord Thomas. Why you think the world of a common thief when you could have Guy Delamar is above and beyond me."

This reasoning had the marvelous effect of conciliating the ladies, but it still didn't quite satisfy their curiosity.

"But where is Delamar?" Lady Lynne asked. "We are only trying to help him. Lord Thomas is a wicked fellow with a pistol. He will certainly have a pistol. If he shoots Delamar, it will be on your head."

"Oh, my God!" Faith gasped. "You're right! Thomas *will* have a pistol! And if he's already stolen, who is to say he won't kill as well?"

"Belle did say he was mean when he was in his cups," Millie said.

"Belle who?" Lady Lynne asked.

"The girl he . . . At the Cranborne Arms, where I work," she said vaguely.

"The lightskirt he was with, is that it?"

It didn't hurt Faith at all to hear in so many words that Thomas was carrying on with the muslin company. Fear for Guy's safety overrode it. "Auntie, we've got to warn Guy," she said.

They both turned to Millie. "Where is he, Millie?" Faith asked. Her voice wasn't hard or demanding or arrogant, but something in her face commanded an answer.

"I don't know. Maggie—that's our madame—figured out where Thomas had the blunt. Guy said he'd be back for it before he hopped the ship and he'd be there waiting for him, but Guy didn't say where it was."

"Then we'll have to talk to Maggie," Faith said calmly.

"You can't go there!" Millie said, deeply shocked.

"Please direct the driver to the Cranborne Arms and tell him to spring the horses," Faith directed.

"Oh, miss, you really shouldn't."

Hard times demanded hard actions. "Do as she says," Lady Lynne decreed, and it was done.

At the Cranborne Arms, Maggie looked with little interest at the hackney cab drawing up in front of her establishment. Private carriages were preferable, and if they had a lozenge or strawberry leaves on the side, so much the better. It was time for her evening girls to be coming home, so the three female heads within caused no surprise. The alarm rose in her breast when she observed that two of the women were ladies. Very few ladies were so enamored of their husbands that they came scampering after them to the Cranborne Arms. In all her years of experience, it had only happened once to Maggie. Once was enough.

She bolted to the front door to waylay them. "Ladies, can I help you?" she asked demurely, then turned a blistering glare on the hapless Millie.

"Are you Maggie?" Lady Lynne asked.

She adopted her most refined voice and said, "I am Miss Maggie Levine. What can I do for you?"

"Tell us where you sent Mr. Delamar. It is a matter of life and death."

"What?"

Millie jumped in, eager to diminish her employer's wrath. "They don't mean to do him no harm, Maggie. It's just that Lord Thomas—well, Belle said he's a mean one."

"The silly chit said nothing of the sort to me!"

"She said it to us girls," Millie insisted. "I'll get her." She ran into the house.

Lady Lynne was curious to see the setup of such an establishment and followed her in against Maggie Levine's most violent protest. It was a great disappointment. She had envisaged red and purple satin, incense burning, women half draped, and other such garish splendors. What she looked at was not much different from any elegant home but newer and in better repair. It was only the few light-skirts adorning the sofas that gave any idea that this was a house of ill-repute. The females were fully clothed but in much grander style than usually seen in the provinces. They were also prettier than most gels. There was much tittering and open-mouthed staring at the feminine intruders.

Maggie herded the ladies into her office and sent for Belle. The girl entered nervously, fearing chastisement. It was clear at a glance that she was not a clever girl. The question had to be put to her a few times before she answered.

"He was all right at first. It was only when he got into the second bottle that he hit me," she said.

"You're supposed to call for help if you run into trouble," Maggie told her severely. "Why do you think I pay three husky footmen to stand twiddling their thumbs all night long?"

"You get mad if there's trouble!" Belle said simply.

Faith felt an awful wrenching of pity in her chest, but time was flying, so she firmed her voice to discover more important items. "Did Thomas have a gun with him?"

"He had a dandy silver-mounted pistol and said he had its twin in his rooms. Nobody was going to stop him, he said. When I asked him stop him from what, he said, 'Never you mind that. That's for me to know.' Mind you, he was real bosky."

Faith looked fearfully at her aunt. "Thomas is a crack shot," she said.

"Give us the address you gave Mr. Delamar," Lady Lynne demanded.

She didn't bother to write it down, and they returned at once to the carriage. Millie had become so engrossed in the affair that she went with them, and the others were so distracted they didn't try to stop her.

"What are you going to do?" she asked Lady Lynne, but it was Faith who answered her.

"We're going to warn Guy."

"He's no flat. He'll be expecting trouble. I think you should go back to your hotel, ladies. I'll warn him for you."

Faith wore a faraway look as though she wasn't listening. Her next question confirmed it. "How old is Belle?" she asked.

"Seventeen, nearly."

"So young to be living a life like that."

"Crikey, I was fifteen when I started! I figure us girls with Maggie are lucky. We live in style. The gents ain't allowed to beat us, we eat real good."

The shadows were lengthening, softening the harsh lines of Millie's face. She looked not only pretty, but also not at all vulgar till she opened her mouth. "How did you . . .

come to—to be a . . ." Faith stammered to a stop, but her meaning was apparent.

"I was hungry," Millie answered. "That's all. I was in the kitchen at Bloeburn Hall, up north of here. They turned me off. I daren't go home. Six mouths to feed—and my pa's got a hard hand. I walked to Bournemouth and met a fellow in the Maze. I stayed with him for a week. He was real sweet, bought me a dandy new dress—silk! I was on my own for a while after he left. You don't get the good customers that way. Sometimes you don't get any. I spent a few nights at Mather's hotel. It's warm at least and the pap isn't too bad. Maggie seen me hanging around the lobby of the theater, trying to pick up a gent, and invited me to join her crew. That was three years ago. I been there ever since. You don't have to feel sorry for me!" she said tartly when she noticed the effect of her tale on the ladies. "I'm better off than most, I can tell you."

"You should go up to London, Millie, and throw your bonnet at a royal duke," Lady Lynne advised her.

"Coo, the likes of me?" Millie scoffed.

"You haven't seen the ugly dumplings they usually consort with. You put them all in the shade."

Millie frowned in perplexity. "That's funny. Guy said you were such toplofty ladies. You're not so bad."

Faith smiled. "You're not so bad yourself, Millie."

The carriage turned on to Poole Hill Road, and Millie pointed out the row of flats ahead. "We'd best not drive up. We should get out and sneak up on foot. It'd be quieter."

"Yes, you do that, Millie," Lady Lynne said. "Faith and I will wait here in the carriage."

"Auntie!" Faith objected. "I am going."

"That you are not, my girl. What would your papa say if I had to take a corpse home to him?"

"And what would *I* say if it's Guy who is a corpse because I hadn't the nerve to warn him?"

"It seems to me you've changed your tune since an hour ago when you were wishing him at Jericho."

"This is different," she countered. "A matter of life and death."

More important to Lady Lynne, it was a matter of nabbing a husband, so she made no further protestations, for, of course, Thomas would not be gauche enough to kill a lady. The carriage stopped, and Millie made one last effort to stop Faith from going with her. It was overborne. The two girls climbed quietly out of the carriage and darted to the side of the street, to proceed in the shadows toward the row of flats across from St. Michael's Church.

"Guy's carriage should be around here somewhere," Faith whispered.

"Lud, he wouldn't leave it standing by to warn Thomas he's here."

"That's true," Faith agreed. She remembered him telling her the same thing back in London. "I wonder where he is."

"You'll never see him. He learned sharp tricks in the Peninsula. He told me about it when he caught the smashers that were working here."

"You've known Guy for a long time, I take it?"

"On and off for a few years, ever since I've been here."

"He . . . frequents Maggie's establishment, does he?" she asked, trying for an air of detachment.

"He might. He never used me, if he does. I met him at the roundhouse when Mather was trying to catch the forgers." She drew to a stop and pulled Faith back by the elbow. She pointed to the top window in the east block and said, "That's it, the flat Lord Thomas has."

"There's no light on. I wonder if they've already left."

"The ship leaves at nine. Guy thought Lord Thomas would come for the money about eight, but he came earlier to be waiting for him. What time is it now?"

Faith squinted at her watch. It was hard to read in the shadow of the trees. "Seven-forty-five."

"I bet Guy's setting there in the dark with his gun pointed at the door. I pity Lord Thomas."

"Thomas can shoot the eye out of a pheasant in flight."

"Go on. Nobody could do that!"

"Yes, he can."

"Lord Thomas will be cautious, too—expecting trouble, I mean," Millie said pensively. "Maybe we should go into the building and creep up the stairs. If Guy hasn't opened the door yet, we could warn him."

A terrible trembling shook Faith at the thought of such danger, but when she spoke, her voice was calm. "I'll go, Millie. Thomas would never shoot me. I might be able to reason with him."

"He could be drunk as a skunk. I'm going with you."

"No, you stay here. Guy may not have gone in yet. We need someone to warn him if he comes along."

"Oh, miss, it don't seem right, sending a helpless lady in there."

"I am not helpless!" Faith said loftily, and walked with trembling knees toward the door of the east block.

Chapter Twelve

It was like entering a tomb to step into the building. Faith's heart pounded mercilessly in fear, and her knees turned to water. The only illumination was pencils of light coming from beneath the doors of the various flats. From beyond the closed doors, the homey sounds of family life wafted down the corridors. A piano was being played in one; a convivial conversation was punctuated by laughter in another. It seemed unreal that ordinary life continued not more than a few yards away. She felt her way to the bottom of the staircase. At the top of the first landing, a faint ray of moonlight penetrated to show her a turn in the stairs.

She listened for a moment, and when no sounds came from above, she began her ascent—slowly, one step at a time. At every step, she thought her heart would burst. She quelled the instinct to turn and pelt back down to safety. Thomas might be there with his silver-mounted pistol aimed this very instant at Guy's heart. She quickened her steps and nearly flew up the second flight.

Once she had reached the top floor, she had to stop and take her bearings. Thomas's flat was in the east corner, facing the street—but was that left or right? She tiptoed to a window at the end of the hall, and when she looked out at St. Michael's, she knew the door nearest to her was the one she wanted. She took a step toward it, listened, and heard dead silence from within. Then she heard a sound from another direction. Someone was coming up the stairs.

It was a slow, shuffling step—an old man or woman. She looked around for somewhere to hide. There was no place— just a door behind her and Thomas's door in front. She leaned back in the shadowed recess of the former and it gave way. She quickly pulled it open and discovered a broom closet. She whisked herself inside, just as the new-comer reached the landing.

She kept the door open just a crack and saw a man continue down the hall toward her. He wore the rumpled jacket of a laborer and a shapeless hat, pulled low over his eyes, on his head. His gait, while still shuffling, was rapid. Her first instant of relief was shattered when he kept advancing past all the other doors to the end of the hall. Good God, he was the janitor! He was coming to the broom closet. She would push the door in his face and run.

She held herself tense to do this. The man stopped right in front of her door, looked around, and pulled out a key. At this close range, she realized he was a bigger man than she'd first thought. When he stood up straight to look around, she rethought his age. He wasn't so old after all. After a short pause, he put the key in Thomas's lock and entered the room. It was all a hum then, that Thomas was in this building. A misunderstanding had occurred somewhere along the line. She had to admit her first reaction was relief, pure and simple. No further show of courage was required of her. She could return to the carriage and . . . And what? Thomas was still at loose, and Guy was still chasing him.

She left the closet and slid quietly into the hall. The old man had closed the door carefully behind him. It was strange he hadn't turned on a light, but no pencil of light showed beneath the frame. While she stood, pondering this, she heard Thomas's voice, and her spine stiffened. ''What the hell!'' was all he said, but it was enough. She'd know Thomas's voice anywhere. He was in there with that old man, and she knew from the rough edge to his words that he was angry. Before she had time to figure out an explanation, a pistol shot rang out. There had been no other conversation. Thomas hadn't waited to ask questions; he had just pulled out his pistol and fired.

And suddenly she knew what it was about the old man that had confused her. It was the latent strength in his shuffle, the way he had straightened up like a young man before inserting his key in the lock. It was Guy! He had donned the disguise to fool Thomas into believing he was a harmless old man, but it hadn't worked. Thomas had shot him, anyway—but was he dead or only hurt? In a blind panic, she put her hand on the knob to open the door, but was stopped by the thump of a body against the wall and the sound of voices. Not dead, then! Thank God he was still alive!

"An old soldier's trick!" she heard Guy say. His voice was silky, calm. "I thought you'd be the sort to shoot first and ask questions afterwards. You're not dealing with babes now, Lord Thomas." A mocking sneer emphasized the title.

She pushed the door open and stared into the dark room. At the far side, there was a man sitting calmly in a chair, not moving. In the dim light from the window, she thought the man was dead, but her greater interest was in the other two. How was it possible that Guy spoke so boldly when Thomas had a pistol pointed at his temple? Another gun hung from his left hand. He stuck it in his pocket. She looked again, shaking her head in confusion, but confirmed that it was Guy, dressed in fustian, who was held at bay. Both men turned to stare when she entered. Somehow, in the few seconds she had waited, Thomas had secured the advantage.

She didn't hesitate a moment before taking a lunge at him. The men were thrown off balance by her entry and didn't stop her. She reached for the gun in his right hand, and at this close range, she saw it was Guy Delamar she was attacking, his feline eyes glaring at her. A tiger looked tame compared to him. Without a second's hesitation, he delivered a sharp blow to the side of her neck. It knocked the wind out of her and she fell to the floor. Then Guy spoke and confirmed that he was not the man in fustian

141

after all. It was Thomas who had donned the disguise—Guy whom she had mistaken for him.

"Sorry to strike a lady," Guy said grimly. More than grimly; there was animal savagery in his voice. "You'd have done better to meet him on board, Lady Faith. Of course you'd have had to make the treacle moon alone, but that would be better than your fate now. Back to the round-house for you."

It was all much too confusing. Guy had hit her, and she doubted she could ever hold her head up again for the ache in her neck. From the floor, she looked aslant at the man in the chair. He must be dead—he still hadn't moved. She looked at Thomas and through the shadows saw a scheming expression settle on his handsome features, only he no longer looked handsome to her. He looked dissipated and hagged and evil. His fustian coat robbed him of even the outer crust of a gentleman, and that was all he had ever had—the outer crust.

"We can talk business, Delamar," Thomas said. Guy gave him a disparaging look but didn't interrupt. "Look, you've got the money . . ."

"A spark of chivalry remains? Lady Faith's freedom for you and the money—is that it? You must remember I am not at all noble in my sentiments, milord, but pray continue."

Thomas hesitated. "That's not the deal. We split the loot. I take half and disappear; you keep the other half and don't let on you ever caught me. A hundred thousand guineas—where else would you ever get so much money?"

"Lady Faith and you continue the jaunt to America?" Guy inquired with mild interest.

"That's up to her," Thomas said, and shrugged his shoulders in indifference.

Faith tried to protest, but her voice refused to form words.

Guy uttered a sardonic laugh. "You'll find it hard to believe, but I'll have more than a hundred thousand guineas of pleasure from seeing you and your lady in the dock. You overestimate both my greed and my poverty. Move. Pick up the girl and walk very carefully out of here.''

Guy picked up the valise of money, put the muzzle against Thomas's back, and watched as he tried to gather Faith in his arms. It was too ghastly, having Thomas touch her. She shook his hands off and struggled to her own feet.

"I can walk," she said in a rough, unnatural tone caused by the blow.

"A squabble in the love nest so soon?" Guy asked, and emitted a bitter little laugh.

"Wait!" Thomas exclaimed. "We can still make a deal. You keep three-quarters of the blunt, Delamar. Just leave me enough to get out of sight. You know a lord will never be hanged. I'll be tried by a jury of my peers—reprimanded—a few years in prison and that's it. Prison isn't so bad for people like me."

"Prison is the only place for people like you!" Guy countered.

"I mean, we are allowed our creature comforts!"

"I am very well aware of the inequities of our legal system. Don't tempt me past endurance, Vane. I'm looking for an excuse to perforate your spleen."

"What difference does it make to *you*? *You* didn't invest anything. You'll still have your story, and a hundred and fifty thousand guineas to boot. You can say I got away with the lot; no one will be any the wiser. Your Mam'selle Ondit can fill a dozen columns with Faith's repinings."

Faith cast one look of loathing at Thomas and rubbed her sore neck. Had she really once loved this groveling, conniving thief who was ready to throw her to the wolves to secure his own freedom?

"Tempting, but I can resist," Guy replied with a jeering lift of his brow at Faith. "Get moving, both of you, with Lady Faith in the lead," he ordered, and Thomas at last moved out of the room, a muzzle nestled against his spine. "Don't try anything, or you're dead meat."

They went downstairs single file. Faith opened the front door of the building and took a step into the street. She looked all around, wondering what had become of Millie, and still wondering about the dead man in Thomas's apartment. Who could he be? She was on nettles to straighten out Guy's misunderstanding of the case but knew this wasn't the moment to distract him. There would be time for that soon enough. The important thing now was to get Thomas under lock and key.

Thomas, very much on his high horse, stopped and asked, "Am I expected to *walk* to the roundhouse?"

"You can crawl on all fours like the cur you are, or I'll be happy to kick you," Guy answered.

They proceeded around the corner, and still there was no sign of Millie. Delamar's carriage was parked a few blocks away. Guy whistled loudly, but the groom didn't appear to hear or see him. The carriage didn't move. They took another step toward it. It seemed the worst was over. No one was looking behind, but it was from behind that a voice stopped them as Elwood suddenly issued from the shadows of a tree.

"Stop where you are. I'll have the blunt," he said.

They turned to see a gun leveled at them. Even while he turned, Guy took aim and shot it out of Elwood's fingers. A loud curse rent the air. Elwood dropped the gun and reeled back, grabbing his wounded fingers. It was hard to pay attention to everything at once, but later Faith realized Thomas must have taken advantage of the momentary distraction to retrieve his gun from Guy's pocket.

Suddenly he had the gun pointed at Guy and pulled Faith in front of himself for protection. "Now the tables are turned," Thomas said. "Throw down your gun and drop the money."

Guy cast a malicious, measuring eye at Thomas and held the gun steady. Faith knew it was only the fact of her shielding Thomas that prevented Guy from shooting and taking his chances. She had never seen such a ruthlessly determined face before. "Don't even think about it, unless you want the girl's death on your conscience," Thomas said. His voice, though frightened, was firm. "Go on, drop the gun." Guy dropped it at his own feet. "Kick it away—far away," Thomas ordered. Guy kicked it off to the side of the road. "Wise chap. Now the valise. Drop it." It fell with a thump. "Now very carefully shove it forward with your foot. You, Faith, reach down and pick it up and carry it. And no tricks, my girl."

Faith looked at Guy. His eyes flickered warily from her to Thomas. She couldn't see the question in them, but surely he was coming to realize she was innocent. She saw the tense, alert set of his shoulders and knew he would take advantage of any help she could give, anything she could do to distract Thomas. Alas, nothing occurred to her. With a gun not six inches from her head, she hardly dared to breathe. Worse, she feared that Thomas would carry her off with him, and once they were alone, he wouldn't be too careful what he did to her.

A low, triumphant laugh bit the air as she retrieved the valise and stood. "That's a good doxy, Faith," Thomas said. "I might take you with me after all—if you weren't such a stiff-rumped little prude. Still, I fancy the girls in America will do me well enough. Now what shall I do with this bothersome wretch?" he asked, and gave Guy a long look. "Simple killing's too good for you, Delamar. You deserve some of the bother you've caused me with your demmed meddling."

Guy's voice cut the air like a knife. "Let her go. This is between you and me."

"Let her go—and have her run to report me to the police?" he asked. "I think not, Delamar."

"Your ship leaves in half an hour. You'll be safe."

"Ships have been followed before and gentlemen removed. We wouldn't want that. I really see nothing for it but to do away with the pair of you."

As they talked, Elwood listened and finally realized there was a gun at his feet. He reached down, picked it up, and placed one throbbing finger on the trigger. Over Guy's shoulder, Thomas saw him and yelled, "Forget it, Elwood. I might as well kill three as—"

Faith thought Guy was looking over his shoulder at Elwood. His head turned, and in the same instant, his foot rose. It came like a bullet aimed at Thomas's gun. The gun flew into the air in an arc and Faith flung herself aside to avoid being hit. She saw the men wrestling, heard the heaving of bodies and the grunts and groans of men locked in mortal combat. When she managed to distinguish individual bodies, she saw Thomas was on the ground, face-down, with Guy on top of him, one hand twisted behind his back so hard she was sure it was broken.

She also saw Elwood standing, watching the struggle, but not taking any part of it. Guy got up and pulled Thomas to his feet. Ever the bounder, Thomas made one last try for freedom. "It was all *his* idea," he said, and pointed to Elwood, but with his left arm. His right hung immobile by his side.

"You're damned right it was, and if you'd stuck to the plan, we'd both be on our way to France instead of to jail," Elwood called back. "But no, you had to have the lot, you greedy weasel."

"You couldn't have raised a penny without me!" Thomas said. "You're nobody. *I'm* the one who made this deal possible. Why should I give *you* half my money?"

"I've heard the last insult from you, my fine gentleman!" Elwood said menacingly.

Faith felt herself being pushed aside, and a split-second later, a bullet whizzed past her ear. Guy had seen what was coming and had saved her. Thomas died quietly. There was just one last moaning sigh as he sank to the ground at her feet. Elwood didn't bother trying to escape. He dropped his gun and straggled forward.

"Good shot, considering I had to use my wounded hand," he said to Guy.

"That wasn't wise, Elwood. Now you're looking at murder."

"I'd have hanged anyway. At least I managed to take

him with me. He was right about his getting off. He'd have dumped the lot in my dish. It's known as British justice.''

"You made your own bed," Guy said, unmoved.

Guy's groom, alerted by the shot, was coming forward now at a fast clip. He hopped down to help his employer.

His toe nudged Thomas, trying to turn him over. "Who is he?" he asked.

"The late Lord Thomas Vane."

"He don't look like a lord."

"He didn't act like one," Elwood said, and got into the carriage, a defeated man.

Guy remained behind for a moment with Faith. She was massaging her neck with her fingers and looked up at him in the shadowy darkness.

"I'm sorry, Faith. I know how you felt about him," he said softly.

Her answer was curt. "No, you don't."

"I do. You're not the first person to have loved unwisely. It only seems unique to each of us. You came to warn him?''

"I came to warn *you*!" she said angrily.

He shook his head ruefully. "You don't have to lie. I have no intention of publicly involving you in this mess." He stopped and looked around at the empty street. "How did you get here? You won't want to climb into my carriage with Elwood and . . ." He looked at the dark form on the ground.

"My carriage is a block away. Millie was supposed to warn you if she saw anything. She must not have recognized a young man in that disguise."

"Millie? So that's how you learned where Thomas was." He turned to his groom. "You keep an eye on Elwood. I'm taking Lady Faith to her carriage."

Millie came panting along the street. "I heard the shot! What happened, Lady Faith? I swear nobody went into the flat except an old gaffer dragging his limb behind him. Guy! Thank God you're safe!" She threw herself into his arms and hugged him.

147

"I'm fine. I got him. See Lady Faith home, Millie."

"Cor, blimey, she don't need any help from me! Full of pluck—for a lady, that is."

When he turned to Faith, his expression was wary. "Yes, I see I've underestimated her gumption." Then he turned on his heel and got into his carriage.

That's all. He didn't thank her, or apologize, or anything. He thought she tried to warn Thomas. She had risked her life for him, and what did she get? A blow to the neck that half killed her and insults.

"What happened?" Millie demanded.

"The old man was Thomas. I don't know what happened, but I think there's a corpse in the apartment."

"Who could it be? Should we report it to Mather, I wonder?"

"Mr. Delamar will report it, I expect. I am going back to the hotel now. I wonder how Elwood got here."

"He must of twigged to it that Tessie was leading him astray and got it out of her somehow. Except Tessie didn't know . . ." Millie thought for a minute. "He must of talked to Maggie. She'd sell her soul for a couple of quid. Of course, he wouldn't let on why he wanted to know. There's no other way he could find out, is there? I'll hear all about it from Guy when he comes to the Cranborne Arms tonight," Millie said.

"Yes, I expect that's where he'll go, all right," Faith said stiffly. Any friendliness she had been feeling for Millie dissipated like a snowflake in a skillet. She was a fool to have tried to help Guy. He didn't need her. He'd have done better without her interference.

Aunt Lynne began pelting them with questions as soon as they entered the carriage. Faith gave short answers till Millie had been let down at the Cranborne Arms.

"What *really* happened?" Lady Lynne demanded then. "I could see you didn't want to speak in front of that young trollop."

"As she said, Thomas is dead. Elwood shot him."

"I made sure Guy would do it. It's the best thing that could happen to poor Thomas now. He'd only have had to kill himself from shame. And Guy got the money, you say?''

"Yes, he has it. You'll get your share back."

"Excellent! I am very happy we came. It was worth it."

"We should have stayed home," Faith disagreed violently. "It isn't over yet. There's a dead man in Thomas's apartment. I have no idea who killed him. We were fools to come on this errand, involving ourselves in this messy business. Mr. Delamar thinks I was there to warn Thomas, that I was planning to go with him to America."

"Egad, you're right! Folks will take the notion you had planned to run off with Thomas, as Guy thought. We must give this careful consideration, Faith, and see if we can dilute suspicion."

"We'll be fortunate if the whole isn't printed up in Mam'selle Ondit's column. I plan to return to Mordain Hall at once."

"No, that would be the end of your chances. You must come back to London and brazen it out. We shall say . . . why, I'll put about the story I took you to the country for a few days to recover from the canceled engagement."

"I wish I *had* canceled it!"

Lady Lynne found this an auspicious moment to say, "You did. I had the foresight, back in Fareham, to realize there was no other way out for you."

"You canceled it without consulting me!"

"Certainly I did. One learns what is best to be done from experience. Why else do you think parents send their chits to me to find them a husband?"

"You should have spoken to me first," Faith said, but she was too relieved to add further animadversions. "In any case, I'm not going back to London. Graveston knows we were with Guy. He saw us."

"He seldom ever goes to London."

"He must at least write to people there. And we told him we were going to Bournemouth."

"Then we must get back to London immediately, this

149

very night. We could be there by tomorrow night if we sleep in the carriage and don't stop except to change teams. If you're seen at a rout tomorrow night, no one will believe you were in Bournemouth today.''

''You're insane,'' Faith said baldly. ''Thomas is lying dead on the ground. I am in no condition to go anywhere, and I certainly wouldn't be able to attend a party tomorrow night after jostling in a carriage for twenty-four hours.''

She might as well have remained silent. Lady Lynne's mind was made up, and her only concern was to iron out any bothersome details. ''We shall attend the Sedgeleys' do. I doubt if word of Thomas's death will have reached London, so we can pretend we know nothing about it or otherwise it would look rather odd, your being at a party. It is fortunate I sent in the retraction of the engagement from Fareham. That should have reached town already.''

''I don't want to attend a party!''

''And you don't want to give Delamar a chance to make it up with you, either, I suppose?''

''I certainly do not!''

''Then you're an even worse ninny than I took you for. Don't be an idiot. This is your chance to nab him. He'd jump at the chance of marrying a Mordain. He has money—he only wants respectability. Why do you think he inveighs so strongly against the nobility? A clear case of blue-blood cholic. He thinks you are above him and is as jealous as a green cow.''

''No, he's not like that. He really hates us.''

''Good! If you'd said he was indifferent, I should be worried. Men always pretend to despise what they really want but think they cannot attain. He'll have you, right enough. He was cutting up at me something fierce for putting forward the match with Thomas.''

''What—what did he say?'' Faith asked.

''Plenty! And your alternative if you once go back to the Hall is to remain there the rest of your life, a spinster.

I should think escaping *that* is well worth twenty-four hours jostling in a well-upholstered carriage.''

"We'll see what Mr. Delamar has to say when he returns to the hotel," she said, half appeased.

"Indeed we shall not. We'll be long gone. He'll have to come calling on us in London. Once he is in the door, we shall have a go at him.''

"We can't just leave Bournemouth without even talking to him," Faith remonstrated.

"I shall write him a note giving him permission to call at Berkeley Square." And permission to pay her bill at the hotel, though she didn't say so.

"But what about Thomas? We can't leave his body here. We must do whatever has to be done.''

"I'll mention it to Delamar" was the solution to this. "It is certainly not *our* place to attend to the mortal remains. Didn't I tell you I have already written the notice canceling the engagement? Thomas Vane is nothing to us but a bad memory now and is best forgotten. It will be for his papa to come pelting down—or perhaps he'll just send word to have the body interred here and keep the shame away from home. Yes, that is what he'll do.''

"I think we should stay," Faith said.

"That is why I am the chaperone and you the charge, because I know what is best to be done and you are a widgeon," Lady Lynne decreed grandly. "If I listened to you, you would now be engaged to a corpse, my girl. Don't forget that. I am leaving with my carriage as soon as I can get my belongings thrown together, and you are coming with me.''

Faith sat scheming the rest of the way to the hotel but could come up with no alternative plan. She knew it was wrong to shab off and leave Guy to clean up the mess, but it was the only way to disassociate herself from Thomas. And if she did not do that, any hope of another engagement was impossible.

She delayed packing as long as she could, in hopes that Guy would return. She even talked Aunt Lynne into the notion of having a box lunch packed to avoid having to stop. That took half an hour longer, but still Guy didn't return. He was at the Cranborne Arms, which suddenly made her aunt's decision to leave the proper one and no question about it. Without further ado, she closed up her valise and announced that she was ready to leave.

Chapter Thirteen

It was all well and good for Aunt Lynne to say Mr. Delamar would call "as soon as he got back." That served as an excuse for the first few days. Faith did not expect him to put himself through the aggravation of a twenty-four-hour uninterrupted jostling in his carriage from Bournemouth to London only from eagerness to see her. He had a few matters to attend to before leaving, they all knew that. Someone had to manage Thomas's funeral, or at least inform his father of the death. There would no doubt be evidence to be presented to Officer Mather and to a magistrate as well.

But when four days had passed and still Mr. Delamar did not present himself at Berkeley Square, Faith fell prey to dire misgivings. Not only did he not love her—he hated her. He was angry, and that man's anger could annihilate her. Should she expect to read the whole unvarnished story in the *Harbinger*? LADY FAITH MORDAIN'S FIANCÉ SLAIN IN ROBBERY ATTEMPT. She would never be able to hold her head up again, or want to, if he did not forgive her. Even Lady Lynne grew impatient with him.

"I'm sure he must be back by now," she declared as the ladies sat in the blue saloon, awaiting the arrival of the latest issue of the *Harbinger*. When the butler brought it in, they both made a grab for it, but it was Lady Lynne who was closer to the door and got hold of it first. After a quick perusal she settled down somewhat.

"There's nothing in the paper yet about the Afro-Gold

affair, so I expect that young Fletcher got this issue out. (Thomas's disgrace was being spoken of in Berkeley Square as the Afro-Gold affair.) The feature story is on the by-election at Fareham and Mr. Shaft's dismissal.''

"I'm sure Mr. Delamar has been in London for days," Faith said. Her jaw took on a certain unattractive firmness as she spoke. "There is no reason to think he'll come hot-footing to see us the minute he arrives. I'm sure I have nothing to say to him, but if he had any claim to propriety, he ought to call on you." She had unconsciously determined that if Mr. Delamar despised her, she would discover no good in him, either.

"He might be spending a few days with Graveston. He said he would stop on his way to London, you recall."

"That would please him, to batten himself on a duke," Faith agreed.

"It would please the duke, that is for certain. Graveston was practically on hands and knees begging him to visit," Lady Lynne replied, and turned the page to her favorite column. "Let us see what Mam'selle Ondit has to say today."

When the lady's only reaction was a few titters, Faith assumed their names were not among those chosen for lambasting. But her calm was soon shattered. "Now here's something interesting! 'Mam'selle predicts there will be a run on silver bullets in the near future when the Peerless Peeress, Lady Marie Struthers, announces her engagement.' He is speaking of gentlemen committing suicide in regret, you see. A bit of whimsy. 'Our congratulations to Mr. D., our best wishes to Lady Marie, and our condolences to the bachelors of England.' Mr.D.! Guy has popped the question, and Lady Marie was not as slow to jump at the chance as *some* young ladies. *That* is why he hasn't bothered to call."

Lady Faith's firm chin wobbled in chagrin. She said not a single word, though her world was in dust and rubble around her. So it was Lady Marie he loved in vain and not a flashing-eyed gypsy. In vain . . . when did Guy Delamar ever do anything in vain? He always succeeded. He had succeeded in destroying her life. She managed to keep her eyes dry and listened to what her aunt had to say on the matter.

She heard a *tsk* of annoyance before the words began. "Well, that is a great pity. I was sure I had attached him for you. *I* did my best. Nabbing a husband requires *some* cooperation from the young lady, however. You must have done something to disgust him, Faith, and I wish you will tell me what it is so that I might warn Hope to avoid it next year."

Faith swallowed and forced herself to speak through the lump in her throat. "I tried to save his life. You must by all means warn Hope to avoid such foolishness."

"Lud, that cannot be it. I told him all about that in my letter. Millie would have explained it as well. He knows it wasn't Thomas you were trying to save. I wonder if our going to the Cranborne Arms gave him a disgust of you. I had not thought Delamar had those squeamish notions of propriety rampant amongst the gentility. No, I am sure he has not. It must be your small dot that held him back. Struthers is giving Marie a fortune—thirty thousand, I believe. Not much we can do about that. Hope has only five thousand like yourself. And speaking of five thousand, when are we to get back our money invested in the Afro-Gold Investment Company? No doubt it will take an age, while the courts discuss it and set up committees to look into it, and meanwhile collect our interest." She set the paper aside and drew a weary sigh. "What time is it?"

"Three-thirty."

"It's a lovely day—weatherwise, I mean. Shall we go for a drive in the park?"

"I'm tired. I'll lie down instead," Faith said.

Her aunt looked at her wan cheeks, her dull eyes, and was stirred to anger. "It is time for some plain speaking, my girl. We have exactly seven days in which to snare you a husband. Dragging around the house like a wounded herb is not the way to set about it. You might sit and sigh for a fortnight and it won't bring him back. You must get out and be seen."

155

The dull eyes flashed to angry life. "I have been seen every night since we got back from Bournemouth! I was seen, half dead with weariness, the very night we arrived. I was seen bored to flinders at Drury Lane the night after that and at the Claymores' ball last night. Short of sticking me in a store window with a For Sale sign, I don't know how you plan to increase my exposure."

"It is not lack of exposure, miss, but the face exposed that is holding gentlemen back. 'Half-dead,' 'bored,' and though you did not add it to your list of expressions, you might well include haughty contempt. It would take a stomach of sheet iron to digest such Friday faces as you have worn from day one, and it gets worse rather than better as the end draws nigh. Fraser stood up with you at the ball last night. I think he might have asked you again if you had not given him your stiff Mordain scowl and gone hiding yourself behind the palms like a timid doe. You must learn to *sparkle*, my dear." She wanted to say "flirt," but to ask a Mordain to flirt was like asking a flower to walk or a cat to fly. It was not in the creature's nature.

Faith lifted her chin and directed a mulish stare at her aunt, but she made no verbal reply. Her aunt noticed her cheeks were burning and would have welcomed a retort, but no, argument was beneath a Mordain. Her tirade was interrupted by the sounding of the door knocker. Both ladies came to rigid attention in the expectation that it might be Mr. Delamar. Dozens of disappointments over the past days had not yet cured them of the habit, but on this occasion their rigidity was repaid. The deep accents of Delamar were heard in the hall, and soon his footsteps advanced toward the saloon. He entered lithely, his eyes darting first to Faith.

Far from sparkling, Faith receded into her shell like an oyster at the approach of the knife. Just having been told she was entirely undesirable, she wanted to melt into the sofa. Failing this, she assumed her usual façade of composure—she looked not only cool but glacial when he made his bows. It was for Lady Lynne to make him welcome and ask all those questions that had been plaguing her.

"Guy! So you are back, you rogue. Have you got my money?"

"It will be returned by the courts in due course."

"That's what I was afraid of. You must scribble up an article for your paper complaining about how they diddle us out of our interest. Come and sit down and tell us all about . . . Bournemouth," she said. She was afraid the words "Afro-Gold affair" might lead him to discuss less interesting matters.

"Thank you," he said, taking a seat beside her and across from Faith. "That's why I'm here, actually. I thought you would be interested to hear the final outcome. I called on Lord Thomas's father, who came to arrange the funeral," he said, staring at Faith, who stared at her lap. His eyes followed hers, and when he saw her ringless finger, a brief smile quivered. "It took a few days, but he managed to pull some strings and got permission to take Thomas home for burial. Of course, the whole thing was a great blow to him. He had some hopes that marriage would settle Thomas down." He was too kind to add the father's suspicion that the unwanted marriage was what had pushed his son over the edge.

"It would have taken more than that to make a silk purse of that sow's ear," Lady Lynne declared vehemently.

Guy looked at the table and saw his paper there, its mussed condition telling him the ladies had been reading it. Lady Lynne followed his glance and said, "we thought we might see something of it in the paper, but I assume young Fletcher got this issue out for you?"

"Yes, he's my assistant editor. This issue is mostly political—the Fareham business."

"Then it is the next issue that will deal with the Afro-Gold affair?" she asked warily.

"I wanted to discuss it with you first. Naturally I don't want to write anything to embarrass—to cause Lady Faith pain." He looked at her, hoping she would return the compliment. The astonished face she wore could hardly be construed as a compliment, but at least she had lifted her eyes from her lap.

"I don't see how that can be avoided," Lady Lynne said frankly.

"The business is over and done with. No one has to know all the sordid details. Thomas is dead, Elwood is in jail—he'll be tried in Fareham—and the money will soon be back in the proper hands. People will eventually hear that Lord Thomas is dead, of course, but the exact manner of his death isn't known to anyone but ourselves and a few discreet people in Fareham. It will likely be assumed he died in a duel or something of the sort. There is no reason to cause Thomas's family unnecessary hurt and shame."

Faith could hardly believe her ears. "But what about your story?" she asked.

"My story will be that the Afro-Gold Investment Company has been dissolved and that the investors will be reimbursed the full amount of their investment. With news like that, I doubt many questions will be asked."

Lady Lynne blinked in astonishment and said, "That's all?"

"I cannot say much more without saying everything. The *Harbinger* isn't in the business of flaying innocent people. The guilty in this case have already suffered. To harp on it would be mere exploitation of the innocent. The less said the better, don't you agree?"

"Certainly!" Lady Lynne agreed, and Faith nodded her head numbly.

"It is the least I can do to repay you for your efforts on my behalf in Bournemouth," he said, again speaking to Faith and wishing the aunt would disappear. "I'm afraid I misunderstood. If I said anything offensive, and I know I did, I want to apologize. I am sorry."

"That's quite all right. I understand," she said in a small voice.

Over a glass of wine, they discussed a few details of that infamous night in Bournemouth. For the most part, Lady Lynne asked questions, Guy answered them, and Faith listened, trying not to look haughty. "You must let us know how much money we owe you for the hotel," she mentioned.

This caused Lady Lynne to change the subject rather quickly. She glanced at the paper, remembered Lady Marie's engagement, and said, "I read that one of your reporters is engaged to a Mr. D. Is it possible that has anything to do with your sudden fit of discretion?"

"No, Lady Marie knows nothing of this business," he said, somewhat confused.

"Perhaps the engagement put you in a good mood, eh?" she persisted.

"I am delighted with the engagement, of course. I expected her father to cast a rub in the way, but he had a blind eye to the groom's lack of a title when he learned the size of his bank balance and that Marie was determined to have him, come what may. She is very modern in her notions."

"That would suit you," Faith said, and looked at him askance.

"I have admired her forever. She'll make a charming wife, but I doubt if she'll continue writing for me. She'll be very busy once she's shackled. A whole house to be done over, if I know Marie."

He finished his wine and set the glass down. Lady Lynne saw no advantage in entertaining a gentleman on the edge of being married and did not try to detain him. Before he left, he drew two white envelopes from his pocket and proffered them, rather hesitantly.

"I am having a rout party tomorrow night to show off my new house. I don't *really* live over my shop, you know," he added jokingly to Faith. "I would be honored if you ladies would attend."

Lady Lynne took the cards. Any party was possible of throwing up a potential husband for Faith, so she accepted. Faith really did not look forward to such an evening at all and objected. "We are promised to dinner with the Hagills, Auntie."

"Why, that is for seven-thirty. We'll be out of there by ten. It will give us a good excuse not to listen to the Hagill gels banging the piano. Tin ears, every one of them, and lead fingers. There's not an ivory on their keyboard that isn't smashed to bits. We shall be very happy to attend your rout, Guy. Where is your new house?''

"I've moved uptown. It's on Piccadilly, bordering the park.''

"Why, you'll be a neighbor to the Devonshires!'' Lady Lynne exclaimed. She had anticipated Upper Grosvenor Square, or some address bordering on good real estate, not at the very heart of it.

"And the Iron Duke, but it was Devonshire who put me on to it. We see a deal of each other in the way of political business, you must know. He'll be attending my party. I look forward to seeing you there.'' His eyes rested on Faith as he spoke. He saw there none of the anticipation he had hoped for, but at least she was coming.

"The Duke of Devonshire, can you top that?'' Lady Lynne said when Guy had left. "And a mansion on Piccadilly. Which one can it be? What a pity we hadn't realized he was a nabob; we might have made a harder push to attach him.''

"He must already have had an understanding with Marie. He wouldn't have proposed without a prior attachment,'' Faith pointed out. But she knew very well that he had spoken of loving in vain. The proposal was new then, since his return.

"Sly puss that she is, offering to garner bits for Mam'selle. Won't she lord it over the world when he sets her up as a neighbor to Devonshire and Wellington! That's why he bought the house, of course, to tempt her. I had thought old Struthers was setting them up in a home. I believe I'll take a run down Piccadilly and see if I can discover which place he bought.''

This errand found favor with Faith. She felt she might as well complete her misery and went for her bonnet. By asking a pedestrian, they discovered which house belonged to Mr. Delamar and drove slowly past it a few times to memorize its façade. It was not quite so large or fine as the Duke of Devonshire's palatial establishment, with eight chimneys visible from the front, statuary, and a stone fence behind the iron palings to obscure the view, but it was still finer than most homes in London. It was a great loss that Faith was not to occupy it.

"They may say what they like of America," Lady Lynne said with a sigh, "it cannot have better opportunities than England, if a fellow is willing to apply himself. Who would have thought it—from a scandal sheet to the top of the hill, and in very short order, too."

A carriage pulled to the door as they drove slowly past, and two ladies descended to enter Delamar's house. "It's Lady Marie!" Faith exclaimed. She looked as hard as she could, but little could be learned from Lady Marie's quickly receding back except that she wore an unexceptionable blue pelisse and a straw bonnet.

"So it is, and her mama, the ugly old cow. They will be arranging Guy's rout party for him. How I should love to have done it. I hope they don't stint on the champagne, eking it out with orgeat as they did at their own do. Still, it is Marie's engagement party and it ain't old Struthers who will be picking up the bill, so we may look forward to some decent refreshment."

With this important detail settled in her mind, she had the carriage returned to Berkeley Square. There were vital decisions to be made. What ensemble to put on Faith to make her attractive tomorrow night. How to drop Fraser the hint, in a manner designed not to frighten him off entirely, that Faith was available. What dessert to order for her own dinner tonight. And, having lost Guy, for a new bridegroom would not be eligible for seduction for a year, whether Mr. Fletcher might be interested in a dalliance.

She hardly noticed that Faith's shoulders were slumped in defeat. She had no way of knowing what was in her mind. Faith was thinking, Mordain Hall, for the rest of her life, while Marie Struthers married Guy. There would be no repetition of that violent kiss. A single kiss in a round-house—that was what she had to remember of love. She felt she could have been the woman Guy chose if only she had not been a blind, proud fool. Surely he had been interested on those few occasions when they had been alone together. But she had disgusted him. He had found her ignorant, and she was—ignorant and unfeeling. She had mocked him and his origins, had shown her shock when she learned he was an officer, had held Thomas up as an example of England's finest, had boasted of her tired blue blood. Of course he hated her. She hated herself. It was a wonder he even asked them to his party.

But he was kind beneath that harsh exterior. He was suppressing an exciting story to spare Thomas's father and herself pain. She had a sad and certain feeling that her life was over. The next decades would be only a decline into old age, lived out in regret for missed chances. How she wished she could turn the calendar back to their first meeting and relive those days. She would praise instead of jeer. She would admit to her lamentable ignorance and ask him to explain the world to her. She would even embrace Whigdom, and for a Mordain that was tantamount to treason. She was in a treasonous, desperate mood. She could never have Mr. Delamar now, but she could at least make him see what he was losing. For one night she could be all those things she had failed to be before. What had kept her locked inside her shell? Shyness—and that was only another name for selfishness. Pride—no virtue but one of the Seven Deadly Sins.

She had been so proud when Thomas chose her over all the other ladies who dangled after him. Had she ever really loved him? Loved—she hardly knew him. She *hadn't* known him. She had never suspected his true nature. If only he had left her picture behind with his prayer book, she would have guessed sooner that he did not care for her. Why had he taken it? How could she have been such a naive fool as to love a stranger? Naive . . . there was the problem, but the scales were lifted from her eyes now. She would listen no more to the urgings of Aunt Lynne but follow her own course.

She was determined to change her ways, and to practice for the performance at Piccadilly the next night, Faith was in lively form at the ball that evening. She entered smiling and nodded at any acquaintances she had made. She stood up twice with Mr. Fraser and did not sit out a single dance.

She chattered like a magpie, and the gentlemen did not appear to care that what she said was largely nonsense. Now if only she had behaved with such liveliness all Season, she would have had half a dozen offers.

Her aunt was at a loss to understand this new mood when it was time to make their toilettes for the Hagill dinner and Guy's rout the next evening. She assumed it was a desperate attempt to get another proposal before her few days were up.

"Not the yellow crape, Auntie," Faith said firmly. There was not precisely a sparkle in her eye; it was more of an angry glitter. "It makes me look like a slab of butter. I'll wear the rose. It is livelier and improves my complexion."

"Your complexion is lively enough, my dear. Quite ruddy for you. You're not running a fever, I hope?"

"No, I'm not," Faith said, setting a pearl barrette amidst her sable tresses. This decking herself out like a dasher was also new. She was happy with the results as she preened before the mirror. She had never looked better, and she knew it.

But Lady Lynne placed her hand on her forehead all the same and was convinced there was an elevation in temperature. "You are dreading the ordeal of Guy's rout party. Perhaps we ought not to attend."

"On the contrary, I am looking forward to it. We did not think to congratulate him on his engagement when he was here yesterday."

"Congratulate him? I begin to think he could have done better for himself than an earl's daughter. Graveston has a sister or two, and there are half a dozen plug-ugly royal princesses desperate for a match. But then Guy is not blind, after all, and the royal merchandise is beyond redemption in looks. Like all young men, he has an eye for a looker. He has got over his disgust of nobility, you see, as I told you he would. It was all a hum to cover up his jealousy. I wonder what title he'll take when they give him a handle."

"Shall we go?" Faith asked curtly. "We don't want to be late for dinner, especially as we mean to leave early."

"Don't mention to the Hagills where we are going,

Faith, in case no one else there has been invited. The Struthers would not have invited the likes of the Hagills and Clarkes to their party.''

''It is Guy's party, and I'm sure he would invite whomever he likes. You sound as though he were a pawn.''

''You're right, of course,'' Lady Lynne admitted.

The Hagills' party was not a great success, perhaps because the ladies could hardly wait to leave it. As soon as Miss Hagill began to drift near the shattered ivories of the keyboard, they made their excuses. Faith was considered brave to enter society at all after jilting Lord Thomas Vane, so no offense was taken at her early departure.

They were silent in the carriage as it delivered them to Piccadilly. A few guests were still arriving at ten-thirty. The mansion was lit from top to bottom, and it made an impressive display towering over the street. An arrow of regret pierced Lady Lynne's heart; she had failed in bringing about this match for Faith. Too late now to nab anyone for her. Her first failure ever. She must do something truly stunning for Hope next Season to atone for it.

The first surprise that greeted the ladies when they entered was the elegance of the house. Guy had spoken of Marie's ''redoing'' it, which was utter nonsense. The second surprise was that there was no sign of the Struthers in the welcoming party. It was that *bon enfant*, Princess Esterhazy, the wife of the Austrian ambassador, who performed the chore of hostess. The princess was known to them from their visits to Almack's, where she was one of the hostesses. Beside her, Guy looked suitably impressive in his black evening suit. It took a real gentleman to look at home in a monkey suit, Lady Lynne always thought. Princess Esterhazy smiled a welcome.

''Lady Lynne, I see you staring to see me hostessing Guy's party. I exacted a stiff price for it. He has promised he will come and make his bows at Almack's. We have need of eligible bachelors there.'' ''Eligible bachelor'' struck the chaperone as an odd way to describe a gentleman halfway to the altar, but it was hardly less surprising than to learn that Mr. Delamar had been urged to attend Almack's, the very pinnacle of London society. The only place higher was the dome of St. Paul's Cathedral.

Lady Lynne passed along the line to Guy. She noticed his lack of ease and put it down to nervousness at his first big do till she chanced to see his eyes sliding off to Faith, who was having a word with Princess Esterhazy. There was an eager brilliance in those eyes, which, coupled with the words "eligible bachelor" and the absence of the Struthers, gave rise to a wild hope. Had she misunderstood the article in the *Harbinger*? Surely his every utterance on the subject had confirmed her suspicions. Yet there was he, smiling like an Ascot winner and hardly able to restrain himself from pulling Faith away from Princess Esterhazy.

She moved along and stood listening while he welcomed Faith. "I was afraid you'd changed your mind," he said nervously. Guy Delamar nervous! She didn't believe it. If that wasn't a man in love, she was a mackerel. "Everyone has been here for an age. You missed the opening dance. I had hoped you would stand up with me."

"We dined out, you remember," Faith said. "We came as soon as decently possible. Your house is magnificent, Guy."

"Better than my loft above the paper at least," he joked, looking around at the expanse of finery. "I'm glad you're not Mr. Delamaring me tonight. Does that mean you've forgiven me?"

"I'm sure if there is any forgiving to be done, it is you who must do it. I only regret I did not thank you properly for . . ." She stopped and lowered her voice. "You know, about Thomas. It was horrid for Auntie and me to shab off and leave you to finish up the mess."

"You did the right thing. That chapter is closed," he said firmly.

Faith noticed the warmth of his regard and fell into a little confusion. "Where is Lady Marie?" she asked, looking around.

"Dancing with her new fiancé, I expect. She and her mama dropped in yesterday and arranged to have the announcement made here tonight, as there were no openings

165

in the social calendar to allow them a party of their own. I am to be Charles Dempster's best man at the wedding, so I am heavily involved in the whole affair.''

"Charles Dempster," she repeated, staring, while realization dawned and a slow smile was born in her eyes. Then he wasn't marrying Lady Marie!

"I see you approve of the match," he remarked. "But enough about Charles and Marie. The guests have arrived for the most part. I can leave the door now. I want to secure a dance before you have the excuse of a full card.''

She felt a joyful fluster and forgot her resolution to be gay and charming. She sounded very like a Mordain when she spoke. "Are you using cards for a simple rout? I thought they were only used at balls.''

"I was speaking metaphorically.''

"Oh, dear, a waltz," she said when the music began. "You know how badly I waltz, Guy. Let us wait for another dance.''

"We'll have a glass of wine instead," he suggested, and led her off to the refreshment parlor. It was busy with guests coming and going, each having a word with their host.

"Why don't we find a quiet corner somewhere?" he asked. "We haven't had a chance to talk. I was wishing Lady Lynne would leave us alone yesterday afternoon.''

Before she could answer, he took her arm and hastened her along a corridor into a handsome drawing room, a little apart from the ballroom and the other guests. His manner, though determined, was nervous—nearly as nervous as Faith's.

"What a lovely room," she said, looking around at the work of Mr. Adams. On the far wall, a marble fireplace gave off a warm glow.

He led her to a sofa, and they sat down. Guy took her glass of wine and placed it on the table beside his own. He said nothing, only lifted his hand and pulled aside the lace shawl that was around her shoulders. His fingers touched her neck. "Ah, I left a bruise," he said softly. "Can you ever forgive me? Beating a woman! You must think me a savage.'' His savage eyes glowed, but his voice was gentle with regret.

Faith felt incapable of speech. A suffocating swelling seemed to be occurring within her. ''It wasn't a beating!'' she objected. Her fingers went automatically to her neck, where they encountered his, and soon the two were intertwined.

''I want to explain—if I can. When you came into that room in Bournemouth, I didn't know how you could be there unless you had arranged it with Thomas. I thought the two of you planned to run off together. Coming on top of my wild-goose chase after the nonexistent Everett Stokely, I was sure you were still in love with Thomas. Then you made a grab for my gun, to convince me. A soldier instinctively protects his weapon. I had struck before I realized . . .''

''I thought you were Thomas,'' she said simply. ''I was in the closet outside the door, and when he came along, disguised as an old man, I thought it was you.''

''Was it really *me* you were trying to protect then?'' he asked doubtfully. ''Millie told me it was so. I'm afraid I've become cynical. I thought you had cozzened her.''

''Belle told me Thomas had two pistols, and was drinking. He was an excellent shot, even when he wasn't sober.''

He smiled, but sadly. ''So am I. I was in the room waiting for him. I knew his reputation as a marksman and took the precaution of having a jacket and trousers stuffed to resemble a man, sitting in the shadows, to distract him. He shot without blinking, Faith. It could have been anyone, though I suppose he thought it was Elwood. Actually, Elwood was scrambling around town finding out from Maggie where Thomas was.''

''Thank God it was only a dummy that was shot.''

''I really don't understand how Lady Lynne could have countenanced such a match,'' he said, his brow clouding angrily. ''I daresay you brought your own subtle pressures to bear on her?''

''I thought I loved him,'' she admitted. ''But not the Thomas Vane you knew, Guy. He had charm and style, wit—oh, I thought him God's gift to womankind, and I wasn't alone in my estimation, either. All the time he was planning this treachery. I am a poor judge, it seems.''

''Folks *do* say love is blind,'' he said forgivingly. His own eyes were alert enough to observe her ringless fingers. ''It seems it makes a lady forgetful as well. We had a wager . . . Do you remember?''

''Yes, the ring,'' she said, and fumbled in her reticule for it. She placed the circle of diamonds on his palm.

He looked at it for a minute, then rose and walked to the fireplace. Without a word, he threw it into the flames. When he didn't return to the sofa, Faith walked over to join him.

''Why did you do that?''

''Because I love you. I'm a jealous, possessive lover, Faith. It will be many a long day before I can remember your loving Thomas without rancor. I don't want any physical reminders of him. For me, there's never been anyone else, you see.''

''What about the Spanish lady?'' she reminded him. A puzzled frown creased his brow. ''The one you loved in vain.''

''She was no Spaniard,'' he said, gazing at her softly. ''I think you know now who I meant. I hoped to get his ring off your finger the day we made the wager. But you were still in thrall to him.''

''No, I just hoped to clear up his thievery quietly.''

''What a vile mess I made of that whole trip. I must have been mad. I can't think why else I've behaved so irrationally—dragging out all my prejudices and ill humor, and finally resorting to physical violence. No, I'm being unfair to myself—perhaps to love. It wasn't loving you that made me so farouche; it was knowing *you* despised *me*, for all the wrong reasons.''

''I never despised you!'' she exclaimed.

''I beg to disagree. You've treated me as an inferior from the day we met, only because I happen to have red blood in my veins and work for my daily bread.''

"I was only afraid for Thomas. I have learned to admire many things about you."

"Admire!" he scoffed. "One admires statues and statesmen, not a lover. I loved you from the minute you walked into my office, looking daggers and speaking them, too. Why else did I put this in my pocket that same night?" he asked, and drew out the ivory miniature she had given Thomas.

"*You* took it!" She looked aghast. "Oh, if only I had known. It was knowing—*thinking* Thomas took it that convinced me he still loved me. I might have been cured ages ago."

He shook his head in regret. "That will teach me to loot."

She took it from his fingers and threw it into the grate with the ring. "There, let that foolish girl burn up, as she deserves to," she said with satisfaction.

Guy was startled at first, then an approving smile glowed. "That foolish girl has spent a few nights in my bedchamber. Can you recommend someone to replace her?"

She gave him a flustered smile. It caused a leap of hope to enter his feline eyes and a new ardor to enter his speech. "Faith, I love you to distraction. I know I've behaved idiotically. I know you're worlds too good for me. Your family will despise me. Everyone will think I'm only trying to scramble up the social ladder, making a hypocrisy of my egalitarianism, and I don't give a damn. I have to know. Will you marry me?"

"Yes," she breathed, and was pulled into his arms for a very tigerish mauling. His lips assaulted hers ferociously, and like any proper lady in love, she returned every assault.

He only stopped kissing her lips to kiss the bruise on her neck, sending a shudder through her body, and to utter recriminations on his boorish behavior.

She didn't answer. His ardent words and hot lips overrode mere rational thought. She only knew she had managed, despite her own folly, to capture the love of a man who was far too good for her. Nothing else mattered. Not

Thomas Vane, not a bruise on the neck. Only this rapturous joy.

"I must learn to control my temper. And I shall," he said firmly. "You have a softening effect on me. I never suppressed a good story before, Faith."

"I like your stern ways, Guy. Don't let the *Harbinger* sink into being just another news sheet. And speaking of the *Harbinger*, shouldn't Mam'selle Ondit be on hand for the Struthers' announcement?"

"The big story in Mam'selle's next column, my sweet, is that Lord Westmore regretfully announces the betrothal of his daughter to Mr. D. If he still acknowledges you as his daughter at all. Will he cut up terribly stiff?"

She was giddy with happiness. "Oh, no, he'll be vastly relieved to be rid of me. Hope is coming on the market next season, you must know, and the law of supply and demand decrees that two Mordains would lower the value."

"There still wouldn't be a *parti* in town good enough for you," he said ardently.

Lady Lynne, curious to discover where her charge had disappeared to, came along the hall peering into rooms for her. When she discovered Faith behaving with such marvelous impropriety, she softly closed the door and went loping after Mr. Fletcher. Or failing to receive any interest on his part, the chantilly creams looked divine.